Beautiful

By Danielle Steel

BEAUTIFUL · HIGH STAKES · INVISIBLE · FLYING ANGELS · THE BUTLER
COMPLICATIONS · NINE LIVES · FINDING ASHLEY · THE AFFAIR · NEIGHBORS
ALL THAT GLITTERS · ROYAL · DADDY'S GIRLS · THE WEDDING DRESS
THE NUMBERS GAME · MORAL COMPASS · SPY · CHILD'S PLAY · THE DARK SIDE
LOST AND FOUND · BLESSING IN DISGUISE · SILENT NIGHT · TURNING POINT
BEAUCHAMP HALL · IN HIS FATHER'S FOOTSTEPS · THE GOOD FIGHT · THE CAST
ACCIDENTAL HEROES · FALL FROM GRACE · PAST PERFECT · FAIRYTALE
THE RIGHT TIME · THE DUCHESS · AGAINST ALL ODDS · DANGEROUS GAMES
THE MISTRESS · THE AWARD · RUSHING WATERS · MAGIC · THE APARTMENT
PROPERTY OF A NOBLEWOMAN · BLUE · PRECIOUS GIFTS · UNDERCOVER
COUNTRY · PRODIGAL SON · PEGASUS · A PERFECT LIFE · POWER PLAY
WINNERS · FIRST SIGHT · UNTIL THE END OF TIME · THE SINS OF THE MOTHER
FRIENDS FOREVER · BETRAYAL · HOTEL VENDÔME · HAPPY BIRTHDAY
44 CHARLES STREET · LEGACY · FAMILY TIES · BIG GIRL
SOUTHERN LIGHTS · MATTERS OF THE HEART · ONE DAY AT A TIME
A GOOD WOMAN · ROGUE · HONOR THYSELF · AMAZING GRACE
BUNGALOW 2 · SISTERS · H.R.H. · COMING OUT · THE HOUSE
TOXIC BACHELORS · MIRACLE · IMPOSSIBLE · ECHOES · SECOND CHANCE
RANSOM · SAFE HARBOUR · JOHNNY ANGEL · DATING GAME
ANSWERED PRAYERS · SUNSET IN ST. TROPEZ · THE COTTAGE · THE KISS
LEAP OF FAITH · LONE EAGLE · JOURNEY · THE HOUSE ON HOPE STREET
THE WEDDING · IRRESISTIBLE FORCES · GRANNY DAN · BITTERSWEET
MIRROR IMAGE · THE KLONE AND I · THE LONG ROAD HOME · THE GHOST
SPECIAL DELIVERY · THE RANCH · SILENT HONOR · MALICE
FIVE DAYS IN PARIS · LIGHTNING · WINGS · THE GIFT · ACCIDENT
VANISHED · MIXED BLESSINGS · JEWELS · NO GREATER LOVE
HEARTBEAT · MESSAGE FROM NAM · DADDY · STAR · ZOYA
KALEIDOSCOPE · FINE THINGS · WANDERLUST · SECRETS
FAMILY ALBUM · FULL CIRCLE · CHANGES · THURSTON HOUSE
CROSSINGS · ONCE IN A LIFETIME · A PERFECT STRANGER
REMEMBRANCE · PALOMINO · LOVE: *POEMS* · THE RING · LOVING
TO LOVE AGAIN · SUMMER'S END · SEASON OF PASSION · THE PROMISE
NOW AND FOREVER · PASSION'S PROMISE · GOING HOME

Nonfiction

EXPECT A MIRACLE: *Quotations to Live and Love By*
PURE JOY: *The Dogs We Love*
A GIFT OF HOPE: *Helping the Homeless*
HIS BRIGHT LIGHT: *The Story of Nick Traina*

For Children

PRETTY MINNIE IN PARIS
PRETTY MINNIE IN HOLLYWOOD

DANIELLE STEEL

Beautiful

A Novel

Delacorte Press

New York

Published in the United States by Delacorte Press, an imprint of Random House, a division of Penguin Random House LLC, New York.

DELACORTE PRESS and the HOUSE colophon are registered trademarks of Penguin Random House LLC.

Hardback ISBN 978-1-984-82164-5
Ebook ISBN 978-1-984-82165-2

Printed in the United States of America on acid-free paper

randomhousebooks.com

2 4 6 8 9 7 5 3 1

First Edition

To my beautiful children,
Beatrix, Trevor, Todd, Nick,
Samantha, Victoria, Vanessa,
Maxx, and Zara,

May the challenges you face be small and rewarding,
May you always be protected from harm,
May you always be safe, happy, and loved,
With all my heart and love,

Mom/d.s.

There will come a time when you
believe everything is finished.
That will be the beginning.
—LOUIS L'AMOUR

Beautiful

Chapter 1

The music was loud and throbbing as fifty strikingly beautiful models pounded down the white satin runner carefully laid out between the chairs meticulously placed in rows. Mirrors reflected the images of the models and spectators. The models intersected with one another in a carefully choreographed pattern at the Chanel ready-to-wear show during Paris Fashion Week in March 2016. The images of the rapidly strutting models mingled with those of the crowd and the bank of photographers captured each moment, each girl, each face in the crowd, showing the collection for the fall.

Véronique Vincent was the first model they saw. She opened the show in a ruby-colored coat, and she was the last in a revealing black velvet gown, which trailed behind her and offered more than just a glimpse of her breasts. She was tall and thin, but not quite as emaciated as some of the others. Many of the girls looked dangerously thin, with severe expressions, flawless makeup, and sculpted hair. The atmosphere was pulsating with excitement, like the music.

Véronique had the smallest hint of a smile as she sailed past the photographers. They knew her well. She was the star of every show she walked in, and had been for the past four years.

She had started modeling at eighteen. She had dark chestnut-colored hair naturally, but let the casting directors dye it any color they wanted. She was famously easy to work with, and a consummate professional at twenty-two. Some of the girls were as young as fifteen. Most were in their late teens, as she had been when she'd started. Véronique had big green eyes, and a ready smile when she wasn't working. Karl Lagerfeld, the famous Chanel designer himself, walked arm in arm with her when he took his bow at the end. She was a favorite of his, and the Chanel show was always the one Véronique liked best. It was flawless, just as she was.

She walked in two or three shows a day during Fashion Week, and she had been dashing from one show to the next for the past four weeks. Fashion Week started in New York with the American designers, and moved on to London for a few days after that to show the work of British designers. After London, Fashion Week went to Milan, and the last Fashion Week was in Paris, for closer to ten days, with a heavy schedule for the most important models. Véronique had the same grueling schedule in September, when the designers in each of the four countries showed their spring lines. Other, lesser designers did presentations in which their clothes were modeled without a fashion show. The runway shows were major productions. They cost millions, and the décor was almost as costly and impressive as the clothes. Chanel was notorious for the most elaborate stage sets, designed by Peter Marino, who sat in the audience watching the proceedings, clad head to foot in black leather.

The runway shows were a spectacle from beginning to end. The audience was comprised of magazine editors, store buyers, famous movie stars from around the world, the wives of heads of state, and illustrious figures from the fashion world. The haute couture shows, which were even more elite, happened in January and July, and Véronique was the star of those shows as well. She had been on the cover of every fashion magazine frequently for the past four years. It wasn't an easy job, and required endurance and hard work. She was often in fittings the night before a show until two A.M. while demanding designers saw to it that each garment fit each model perfectly. There was pandemonium backstage at every show, while stage managers from the design houses oversaw every detail, and in some cases dressers stripped a model and redressed her in a matter of seconds, with all new jewelry and accessories to go with the change. Only their hair and makeup remained the same.

Véronique took it all in stride. None of it was new to her after years of the same routines. During the rest of the year, she was constantly in photo shoots all over the world, and had worked with all the most important photographers. She was always in high demand, and had thrown herself into her career wholeheartedly, knowing that the crest of the wave wouldn't last long. One day it would be over. She had made a lot of money, and turned it all over to her mother, who had a good head for business and invested it well. Véronique had total confidence in her. Her mother, Marie-Helene Vincent, was a lawyer, and Véronique was unusual in how close she was to her mother. Many of the young girls from Eastern European countries came to Paris unprotected to seek their fortunes, modeling for as long as they could, and hoping to find a man to marry or support them. The men who pursued supermodels were a special breed, addicted to beauty, wanting a young girl on their arm. Some of them were extremely generous, others less so. They used the girls as accessories to enhance their image. Many of the girls got into drugs once in the fast lane, but Véronique never had.

Her beauty had been striking since she was thirteen. Men in the street stared at her, others tried to hustle her. She had been well protected and carefully brought up by her mother, who had insisted that her education came before her modeling career. For the first two years of her career, she had attended the Sorbonne part time, and majored in art history and French literature. She was halfway to a teaching degree she intended not to use until she was much older and had no other options. In the meantime, she had recently been the face of a well-known cosmetics line, and before that the face of a perfume. Jewelry houses clamored to have her in their ads, and she had been the primary model for an airline for a year. She never lacked for assignments, and had to juggle them all. She was part of an industry in which she was the commodity she was selling.

Her mother was relieved that so far none of it had gone to her head, despite so much attention focused on her. Véronique treated it like a job she was serious about, and never let herself be distracted, as many other girls did, their heads turned by their own beauty. Her mother always reminded her that external beauty was fleeting and real beauty came from within. It was part of her now, like a hand or a leg. Her exquisite face was just another body part, and it served her well. She didn't dwell on her looks, and never thought of herself as others did. She was paid well for what she did, like a gift she had received and had done nothing to acquire. She considered her beauty an accident of fate, like a beautiful singing voice, or the ability to paint. Her exceptional looks had turned into a lucrative career.

She had paid no attention to it at all when she was younger, and to her it was simply a job. Modeling had opened doors for her, and she was well aware that she couldn't take the men who pursued her seriously. She had no desire for a lasting relationship at her age. She had fun with the men she went out with, but their relationships never lasted for more than a few months. She was invited on yachts and on corporate trips by the companies she worked for. She was sometimes paid to go to parties for publicity purposes, and she never lacked for men to go out with. Her current "date" was Lord Cyril Buxton, handsome, from an excellent British family, and twenty-seven years old. He was meant to be working for his father at a bank in London, but spent far more time playing in Paris, and with her, and avoided his family as much as he was able to, much to his parents' chagrin. Véronique had met them once when she was doing a shoot for British *Vogue* in London. They were grateful that their son wasn't dating another greedy Russian model who was looking for a rich husband, but they weren't warm to her. They wanted him to fast-forward through this stage of his life and get serious about his work and grow up. He had no interest in becoming responsible and giving up his fun life or dating the women they thought he should. They wanted him with a British aristocrat like himself.

Cyril had as little interest in marriage as Véronique did. She wasn't sure she'd ever marry. It seemed like an overwhelming commitment to her. Her parents hadn't been married, and it had never bothered her. Her father was American, also an attorney. Her mother had met him while at a legal convention in New York. They had had a passionate affair for two years, until Marie-Helene got pregnant at forty-one, and realized it might never happen again. She decided to have the baby with Bill's consent. She was forty-two when Véronique was born, and Bill Smith was sixty-one. He had died in a car accident when Véronique was six months old. Marie-Helene didn't like to talk about it, and never told Véronique the details of her father's death, only that he had died instantly in a car crash somewhere near New York, when a truck hit his sports car on a rainy night. So she had never known her father, only that her parents had loved each other deeply. She had grown up happily alone with her mother, and Véronique had always said that you couldn't miss what you didn't know. She knew her father only from the photographs around their apartment, several in her own room, and the stories her mother told her about him, and how in love they had been. Véronique knew it was true since there had never been a serious man in her mother's life after him, and she could see from the photographs that he was a handsome man. Once in a while, she wondered what it would be like to have a father, when she saw her friends enjoying a special moment with theirs, but most of the time she was content with her mother, and spending time occasionally with her friends' fathers growing up. They'd had a brief bumpy time when Véronique was in her early teens, but that ended quickly, and both women readily admitted that they were best friends. They were proud of how close they were, and respected each other.

Véronique always sought her mother's advice, and trusted her wise counsel, except about men. Marie-Helene still complained about the kind of spoiled, self-indulgent men Véronique dated. They were always after her for the wrong reasons, because of her fame as a supermodel, not for who she was as a person. But Véronique didn't mind. She had fun with them, which was enough for now. She had her own apartment on the rue de l'Université in the fashionable seventh arrondissement on the Left Bank, which her mother had let her buy at twenty-one as a good investment. It was small, and useful for her to have her own place, but on weekends when she had no plans, she often stayed with her mother in the quiet, staid, residential seventeenth arrondissement where she had grown up. It was an upper middle class neighborhood for bourgeois families. Marie-Helene worked very hard in her law practice, and kept long hours too. They were both hardworking women, with an unusually strong work ethic.

Her mother was sixty-four now, and hadn't had a man in her life in a dozen years, and no one she had ever loved as she had Bill. With Véronique and her law practice, she said she didn't have time, nor the interest. Véronique had asked questions about her father as a child, but Marie-Helene didn't like to talk about him. She said it made her too sad since his untimely death, so Véronique learned not to press her about it, and didn't want to upset her, even now that she was grown up. She didn't want to make her mother uncomfortable, and she knew as much as there was to know about her father, that he was American and a lawyer, and sixty-one when she was born. She had never asked her mother why they didn't marry. Several of her friends had unmarried parents while she was growing up, and it wasn't considered unusual or shocking, so that didn't bother her.

Marie-Helene's parents had been straitlaced, old-fashioned aristocrats with very little money. The family chateau, art, and furniture had been sold even before Marie-Helene was born. Her mother had never worked, her father worked in a dignified, small private bank in Paris. They hoped Marie-Helene would marry well one day, one of their own kind, and were unhappy when their daughter chose law as a career, but it had been lucrative for her. They hadn't lived long enough to know that she never married and had had a love child, which would have horrified them. Véronique never knew her grandparents. The only relative she had in the world was her mother and it was enough for her.

They didn't live extravagantly, but they lived nicely. Their apartment was genteel but not luxurious, and big enough for the two of them. It was decorated mostly with Marie-Helene's parents' remaining antiques. Véronique had no hunger for the glamorous life her own career could have provided her, and although she attended major social events in the fashion world, and had an apartment of her own, she was just as happy spending a quiet weekend relaxing and watching TV with her mother in the apartment where she grew up, that had always been home. It seemed perfect to her, and a safe refuge from the fast-moving world where she worked. Her mother was pleased that Véronique's success hadn't spoiled her, and she was always happy to come home. Her own small apartment never felt like home to her.

*   *   *

Véronique undressed quickly as soon as she came off the runway, and pushed her way through the crowd backstage to a small changing room where she had left her jeans and T-shirt. She pulled on motorcycle boots and called her mother before she left the Grand Palais, which was a magnificent Victorian glass structure where many fashion shows were held, as well as antique fairs and art events.

Marie-Helene answered on the first ring, as soon as she saw Véronique's number come up.

"How was it?" she asked, always pleased to hear from her. She knew how busy her daughter was during Fashion Week, and didn't expect her to call. She never attended the shows herself, which were by invitation only to the fashion elite, but she watched the videos online of every show Véronique was in.

"It was fine, nothing unusual," Véronique said. "How are you?" In the madness of Fashion Week, they hadn't spoken in two days, which was rare for them. They normally spoke at least once a day.

"I'm fine, crazy busy too, though not as busy as you are." Marie-Helene smiled. She had seen the madness of Fashion Week at close range while Véronique had still lived with her. She missed that now that Véronique had her own apartment, although she came home frequently, for a meal or to spend the night when she had nothing else to do. "I have to go to Brussels next week. I'll probably be there for about ten days. You can come and see me if you have a break." There was a fast train that got to Brussels from Paris in an hour and twenty minutes, and residents of both cities went back and forth with ease, for business or social events. Marie-Helene had several clients there, since many wealthy families had moved to Belgium and Switzerland when the socialists came into power in France, and the rich began to leave to avoid punitive high taxes. So she went to Belgium frequently to see long-standing clients there.

"I'm booked solid for the next two weeks, with magazine shoots," Véronique told her. "I could come after that if you're still there."

"Let's do that, and then go somewhere for a few days. It would do us both good."

"I'd love it. I've got a shoot in Tokyo for *Vogue* after that, but I've got a window in between. It would be fun to get out of here and get some sun. I haven't come up for air in a month," Véronique said, glancing at her watch. "I've got to go, Mom. I've got a mototaxi waiting outside. I've got to be at my next show in half an hour for hair and makeup."

"I wish you didn't take those damn motorcycle taxis. They're so dangerous," Marie-Helene complained.

"It's the only way I can get around on a tight schedule." Her mother knew it was true.

"How's Cyril, by the way? Is he here?" Marie-Helene asked her.

"Of course." Véronique laughed. "He wouldn't miss Fashion Week. We went to a party Chanel gave two days ago, and Dior is giving one tonight. I just want to go home and go to bed, but I know he'll be upset if I don't go." He loved being seen and being in the press with her. It didn't bother her. It was part of the territory, and came with who she was. He wouldn't have been dating her if she weren't a supermodel. It annoyed her mother, but Véronique didn't care. They had a good time together. There was a carefree boyish side to him she thoroughly enjoyed. He acted like a kid at times.

"Well, try to get a little rest here and there, and eat occasionally.

I'll start thinking about where we can go for a few days. Maybe Miami. It's easy to get to, and warm this time of year." Saint Bart's and the Caribbean were more of a scene and Véronique would be recognized everywhere, which wouldn't be restful for her. Her face was well known around the world.

"I love you, Maman," Véronique said hurriedly, put on a warm jacket, and rushed out, pushing her way through the still heavy crowd backstage. She left through a stage entrance, and saw the motorcycle taxi waiting for her, along with several others. He had driven her there earlier. All the models were in a hurry to get to the next show they were booked for. She rushed over to the driver, as a group of photographers pressed toward her. She put on the helmet the driver handed her and hopped on, and the photographers took rapid-fire photos of her as he started the bike and they made their escape through the Paris traffic. She was at her next location ten minutes later, in record time, and the madness started all over again with another fashion show.

Cyril was at the second one, seated in the second row. He helped her leave afterward in the chauffeur-driven Bentley he had hired to attend the show and was keeping for the evening, to take them to the Dior party. It was being held in a private mansion Dior had rented for the occasion.

Véronique was exhausted when they got back to her apartment after the show. She'd been running all day, and for weeks. She'd gotten to bed at three A.M., after fittings at Chanel. The sewers had worked all through the night on final touches, and she'd been up at six for fittings somewhere else.

"If I lie down, I might die," she said to Cyril, as he handed her a glass of champagne. "I don't suppose you'd want to stay home to-night," she said hopefully, and took a sip.

"Of course not. Don't be silly. We can't miss the Dior party." She would have been happy to, but didn't want to disappoint him.

She wore a fabulous red satin gown they had lent her, which molded her body, and brushed her long chestnut hair loose down her back. She felt like she was sleepwalking by the time they left her apartment, and she almost fell asleep in the Bentley. But she came alive again when they got to the party. She had to admit, it was fun. She saw lots of people she knew, and she and Cyril were photo-graphed constantly while they were dancing and he was delighted. They left the party at midnight, and he wanted to go dancing at a club.

"I can't," she said, stretching her long legs in the back of the lim-ousine. "I have to be up again at six tomorrow." Fashion Weeks were always like that, a mad dash of shows in the daytime, and an end-less round of parties at night, and Cyril didn't want to miss a minute of it.

"You work too hard," he said. "My father called today. He wanted to know when I'm coming back. I almost told him 'never.' He's get-ting cantankerous about my being here. I've only been in Paris this week for heaven's sake." He hadn't been to Milan with her, although he had come to New York for the shows she was in there. "A boy's got to have a bit of fun," he said, kissing her lightly on the lips. But he usually had quite a lot of fun, much to his parents' dismay. It was difficult to pretend he even had a job. Since he worked for his fa-ther, he felt he could do whatever he wanted. "What are you doing after the madness is over?"

"I've got two weeks of shoots booked, and my mother just invited me to go away with her for a few days. I think I might do that."

"Oh, fun! Can I come? I love your mother." He was like a big kid, or a large unruly dog wagging his tail. It was hard to get angry at him. He was exuberant and lovable, although Véronique wasn't in love with him, but she liked him a lot.

"No, you cannot come," she said, laughing at him. "You'll keep me out all night, wanting to go to parties and nightclubs. I want a couple of days of downtime with my mom. I work a hell of a lot harder than you do, and I need a break." He looked mildly disappointed as they arrived at her apartment, and he poured them both another glass of champagne when they got upstairs. Véronique didn't touch hers, and went to get ready for bed, while he enjoyed the view of the Eiffel Tower and finished his champagne.

She was already in bed by the time he walked into her bedroom and sat down on the bed next to her. He kissed her amorously, and tried to inspire her. She smiled sleepily at him.

"I had fun tonight," she said. She enjoyed her time with him, and loved dancing with him. She just couldn't party all the time the way he did, and didn't want to. She worked too hard to be out every night, a concept he never understood. At twenty-seven, he wanted to have fun all the time. He came to Paris for that, not to sleep.

"We should have gone on somewhere to go dancing," he said and kissed her again.

"You're trying to kill me," she said, and he laughed.

"Definitely not. You're way too much fun. Why would I want to kill you? Back in a minute," he said then, and headed for the bathroom. He had been drinking steadily all night, but he was never disagreeable, even when he was drunk, and he had an amazing tolerance for alcohol. He was always a gentleman, no matter how much he drank.

He was back two minutes later, had taken off his jacket and tie and was unbuttoning his shirt. She was in bed with her back to him, and he kissed her back and her neck, and was surprised when she didn't respond. He bent over her, and kissed her with mounting passion, and then saw that she was sound asleep. It had been a very long day for her, and an endless four weeks.

"Oh well," he said with a smile, and walked back out to the living room to finish the bottle of champagne. Véronique was dead to the world.

Chapter 2

Cyril spent the next two weeks in Paris with Véronique. He slept late, got massages, and had lunch with friends while Véronique went to her photo shoots and honored her commitments. They met at night to have dinner or go to parties she was invited to, or that he'd wangled invitations to on his own. Knowing she would be with him, people invited him to everything nowadays. She was his entrée to the most elite, closed jet-set circles, and even though she worked long hours at the shoots, it was much less demanding and stressful than the fashion shows were, and she was game to go out with him in the evening. His father was fuming in London, and Cyril didn't care. He was a spoiled only son, who had not lived up to their expectations yet, and maybe never would. Véronique was used to men like him, who behaved more like boys. He wasn't much older than she was, only five years. He loved to have a good time, and was addicted to beautiful women. It was a breed that was familiar to her, the men who chased supermodels. Cyril was a prime example.

Cyril said openly that Véronique was the most beautiful girl he had ever known, and she was smart too. She saw right through him, which he found amusing. There was no artifice to Cyril. He never pretended to be something he wasn't, and he never made promises he couldn't keep. He lived by an honor code according to his up-bringing, which in his case didn't include work. He had no desire to grow up, and wanted to play for as many years as he could get away with. She made no demands on him, and didn't want anything from him materially. As far as Cyril was concerned, she was the ideal woman, and they had the perfect relationship. Even her mother couldn't get too angry with him, although she deplored his lack of work ethic, but he was just an overgrown child in a handsome young man's body, with no malice to him, and he treated Véronique well. He was a gentleman and a kind man.

Véronique's plans to go away with her mother had firmed up, and they were both looking forward to it. They had decided on Miami, which was just glitzy and corny enough to appeal to both of them, and the shopping was great.

"That's not fair," Cyril complained, when he heard Véronique make plans with her mother on the phone. "I want to come too."

"You can't," Véronique said bluntly, laughing at him, "unless you want your father to kill you or disinherit you."

"Oh, that. He takes things much too seriously," Cyril said light-heartedly. "Why don't I at least come to Brussels with you for the night? I'll invite you and your mother to dinner, and we can all go to the airport together the next day. I'll fly back to London, and you and your mother can go to Miami, and abandon me to freezing London weather and my dreary existence at home. I'll come back in a few weeks. Or will you be away then?" He could hardly keep up with her schedule.

"I'm going to Tokyo after Miami, but after that I'll be home for a few weeks." She enjoyed the trips for photo shoots as long as they weren't too dangerous or in very primitive places.

"I wish I had your life," he said enviously.

"No, you don't, I work much harder than you do," she reminded him, and he didn't deny it.

"You get to play a lot too," he reminded her. But he also knew that she went out less than most of the models he had met, those who were looking for a good time and a wealthy man. Véronique was impressively self-sufficient, and she expected nothing from him. He suspected she wouldn't cheat on him, which was rare in her world too. Morals tended to be fast and loose in the crowd they both moved in. She was undemanding, always fun to be with, intelligent, and spectacularly beautiful. It was all he wanted in a woman. He even liked her mother, a direct, honest, open, incredibly bright, inter-esting woman, who had had a long, impressive career in the law. He liked talking to Marie-Helene more than he did his own mother, who complained all the time about how difficult the servants were, how hard his father worked, and how much time he spent hunting and at his club. They gave a lot of weekend parties at their country estate in Kent, which bored Cyril to tears.

With no objection from her mother, Véronique agreed to let Cyril come to Brussels with her for the night, and they all planned to leave early the next day, heading off in opposite directions.

Véronique and Cyril took the fast train to Brussels on Monday afternoon. She dozed on the train and he answered emails on his computer. He sent Véronique an email telling her he loved her, and she smiled when she saw it on her phone when she woke up. He caught up on news and read that the main terrorist responsible for the November attacks in Paris had been arrested in Brussels two days before.

They were both in high spirits as they took a cab to the apartment where Marie-Helene stayed when she worked in Brussels. She was concluding her work that day, with her last appointments with her clients, and she was going to meet Véronique and Cyril at the apartment by dinnertime. Véronique had already complained that they were taking such an early flight to Florida and had to check in at eight A.M. the next day, but Marie-Helene didn't want to waste a minute of their mini-vacation. They were only planning to stay in Florida for three days.

"It works for me anyway," Cyril assured her. "I'll get to the bank early, so my father won't be pissed at me."

Véronique set the table for her mother when they got to the apartment, and Cyril had brought a bottle of very fine red wine. Since they had to get up early, they had decided to dine at home. When Marie-Helene got home, she had bought foie gras and a cooked chicken and some sausages, and they had an easy, casual dinner in the small kitchen. Cyril had generously offered to take them to a nice restaurant, but it was easier to eat in. They had a lovely evening, chatting in the kitchen, and Cyril made them both laugh with tales of his parents' house party hunting weekends. "I avoid them whenever possible. They're positively, deadly boring," he said, as they finished his bottle of excellent wine.

Marie-Helene was elated to be going away with her daughter, and Véronique was excited too.

"I'm going to look like a slob all weekend," she warned her mother. "I don't care who takes my picture. I don't want to see decent clothes for the whole three days. And I warn you, Mom, I'm traveling in my worst old jeans."

Her mother smiled at her. "I don't care if you travel in your pajamas. I'm just happy we could both find the time to get away together." Marie-Helene had planned it carefully to make the time.

"Stop talking about your trip!" Cyril grumbled, as they cleared up after dinner. "I'm green with envy. I'm going back into slavery in grisly, dark, freezing cold London. It's in very poor taste for you two to gloat about it. You have no compassion whatsoever."

"No, I don't," Véronique said as she kissed him, "I've worked my ass off for the past six weeks." Her mother worked hard too.

They all went to bed early, Cyril and Véronique in the apartment's second bedroom, and met in the kitchen the following morning at six, while Marie-Helene made coffee and toast for all three of them. They were all half asleep, and no one chatted as they had the night before. They went back to their rooms to shower and dress, and were ready right on time. Marie-Helene and Véronique with a small suitcase each to check in, and Cyril was wearing a proper business suit, white shirt, Hermès tie, and a navy cashmere overcoat. He looked very handsome.

"You look very nice when you go to work," Véronique complimented him as they got into a cab to go to Zaventem Airport.

"Thank you," Cyril said glumly, and looked as though he wished he were going anywhere but back to London. Marie-Helene and Véronique were speaking softly to each other about their trip. He had a small suitcase with him too, and had left some clothes at Véronique's apartment in Paris. He carried the bags into the terminal for them, and accompanied them to their check-in, in true gentlemanly fashion. He had time to get to his own plane after that.

"That's very sweet of you," Marie-Helene thanked him, as they stood in the check-in line together. It was five to eight, and they were perfectly on time. He stood patiently behind them with the bags.

"What do you think if we . . ." Véronique said to her mother, and never got to finish her sentence. As she said it, at two minutes to eight o'clock, there was the sound of a massive explosion. A bomb exploded several feet from where they were standing in the departures terminal. The bomb blew a huge hole in the building, as parts of the roof and beams came crashing down on them. Twisted metal and broken glass rained on the waiting passengers in line. People were screaming and running in all directions to get away from the heart of the explosion. Within seconds, a second bomb exploded at the other end of the departures terminal. There were bodies and injured people on the floor everywhere, some of them with huge pieces of steel lying on top of them, several of them obviously dead. Dark smoke was heavy in the air. Véronique looked around her to find her mother and Cyril, and couldn't see them anywhere in the thick black smoke that surrounded them, and then she realized, when she tried to run, that she was lying on the floor under a heavy slab of metal that was crushing her. She could not move or go anywhere or even make a sound. She could hear screaming and shouts in the distance, and sirens shortly after. She couldn't feel her body, and was dazed and in shock. No one could see her where she lay and no one came to her aid. All she could do was hope that Cyril and her mother were okay. She felt strangely light, as though she were floating, and the sounds around her faded into the distance as she drifted in and out of consciousness. She kept waiting to hear her mother's voice near her, and called out to her a few times, but no sound came from her mouth, as she lay under the beams and pieces of the roof of the terminal.

It seemed like hours before she heard voices coming closer, but it didn't sound like her mother or Cyril. They were men's voices. She felt her body get even lighter and she was sure she was floating away, and then there were bright lights in her eyes, but she couldn't distinguish forms or faces. She wondered if she was dying or had already died. She heard a voice speak distinctly in French.

"No, she's dead," someone said decisively, and then she felt hands on her neck and heard more shouting. Whoever they were talking about was alive and not dead, and she had no idea who it was, and had no awareness that they were talking about her.

She heard heavy metal grinding sounds, and machinery that sounded too loud in her ears, and the weight she had felt for what seemed like hours lifted off of her, and someone said, "Oh my God . . ." and then she felt herself being lifted up and laid down somewhere. It didn't hurt when they moved her. She was completely numb. A woman's voice asked her name and she told them.

"My mother . . . Cyril . . ." she whispered, as she had the sensation of flying or moving very quickly, as the paramedics put her on a gurney and rushed her to an ambulance. She was covered with blood, with shrapnel wounds covering her entire body, which she wasn't aware of. The clothes she had worn were only shreds after the explosion. The floor around her was littered with hundreds of injured, moaning people, and body parts, which had flown through the air and landed helter-skelter everywhere.

She had no way of knowing that a third bomb had exploded at Maelbeek metro station an hour after the attack at the airport. Sixteen people lay dead at the airport, and another sixteen at the metro station. Between the two locations, first responders were dealing with three hundred and forty severely wounded people, with unimaginable injuries from the homemade bombs, made of household chemicals and peroxide and filled with nails and bolts and pieces of metal to intentionally tear bodies apart and cause even greater harm than just from the explosion. There was so much blood on Véronique's face that no one could have identified her, even her own mother. Their bodies had not been identified yet, but Marie-Helene and Cyril had been killed instantly in the first explosion and their bodies still lay beneath the rubble. It was a miracle that Véronique had survived it. She looked so severely damaged and so lifeless that the paramedics on the scene were sure she was dead when they lifted the piece of the roof off of her. They were certain that she had suffered countless broken bones and massive internal injuries, and her face was unrecognizable under all the encrusted blood, with gashes all over her face and body. She was lying almost naked when they discovered her. She slipped into unconsciousness as soon as she whispered her name in answer to the question.

Like the rest of the wounded, she was taken to a nearby military hospital, which was better equipped to treat injuries of this nature.

These were wartime injuries, from massive explosions, normally never experienced by civilians. Véronique was one of the last to arrive at the hospital, and was rushed into surgery immediately. There were people on gurneys crowding the halls, waiting for rooms and operating rooms to open up, as nurses and doctors did triage up and down the halls. Less severe injuries were being treated by paramedics, but there were very few minor injuries. Most were very extreme, with some of the victims burned on their entire bodies, and others who had suffered severed limbs. One woman had lost both arms and both legs. Children were being treated as a priority.

Belgian officials had sprung into action. Three suicide bombers died in the explosions, but they had taken thirty-two souls with them, and injured over three hundred others. It was a massive terrorist attack on Brussels. The police had been following leads on other terrorists concealed in the city, but had not succeeded in rounding them up and stopping them in time.

Véronique spent seven hours in surgery that night, to remove the vast quantities of metal and shrapnel that had entered her body. It would require many operations, but they attempted to remove the most acute pieces, which were the most dangerous and were threatening her arteries. She was categorized at the highest degree of critical, and never regained consciousness again after giving her name. The surgeons worked diligently to save her, and to treat the deep lacerations on her face.

Bernard Aubert was sitting in the office he had shared with Marie-Helene Vincent for thirty years. He had first heard the news of the attack in Brussels on his way to work that morning. He knew that Marie-Helene had been in Brussels for two weeks, but assumed she would be taking the high-speed train back to Paris. She had told him she was taking the rest of the week off, but hadn't told him she was going to Miami. Unlike Véronique, she hadn't been carrying a purse, but had a belt with a money purse around her waist, with her passport in it, and since he was listed as the person to notify in case of emergency on her official papers, the Brussels police called him that afternoon.

Bernard was sixty-five years old, and had been divorced for years. He was planning to retire at the end of the year, and had told Marie-Helene his intentions a few months before. They had been practicing law in their shared practice for thirty years. He considered her a close friend, and had a deep affection and respect for her, and he was in shock when they told him that she had died at Zaventem Airport. They questioned him about another victim with the same surname. They said that they had a Véronique Vincent at the hospital, listed as severely critical. She was still in surgery at the time.

"Oh my God, that's her daughter. I didn't know she was with her." They told him that he would be kept closely informed, but if she survived, the doctors' intention was to put her in a medically induced coma after the surgery, and she was expected to have more surgeries in the next few days. He was shaking when he hung up, and burst into tears. He couldn't believe what had happened, that Marie-Helene had been killed and Véronique was fighting for her life. Since she wasn't conscious, he decided to wait before he went to Brussels. He could offer no comfort or help in the circumstances.

Their secretaries and paralegal, and a junior associate who was working on some of their cases, all moved around the office as quietly as they could, devastated by the news. Bernard looked gray as he sat at his desk, alternately crying and staring into space. It was a cruel end for his colleague and dear friend, and even more tragic if her daughter died too, at twenty-two.

The reports on television of the bombings were harrowing, with terrifying photographs of the departures terminal after the two bombs exploded, and the metro station. A third bomb had been found at the airport, which hadn't detonated. A terrorist group had claimed responsibility for the attack, which was believed to be tied to the November attacks in Paris four months before.

Bernard waited until the next day to go to Brussels, and was only permitted to see Véronique for a few minutes, in the intensive care unit. She was deep in a controlled coma after the surgery. He spoke to the doctor in charge of her care, and was told that her survival was still gravely in question. Her body was still full of shrapnel, some in critical locations. They had removed as much as they could for now, but by no means all. And if she did survive, she would do so with some shrapnel in her body forever. Removing some pieces of it was just too dangerous. She was at risk for losing an eye as well. Bernard saw that her face was heavily bandaged, and the doctor told him that she would need reconstructive surgery for the damage to her face, and she had suffered internal damage to her vital organs as well. He cried again while listening to the doctor, and knew how heartbroken Marie-Helene would have been to know the condition her daughter was in. The doctor estimated that she had a fifteen to twenty percent chance of survival, but was not optimistic. The only thing in her favor was that she had youth on her side, which would help her recover if she survived her injuries. The people who had built the bombs had maximized the damage they would cause to the human body, and had done so very effectively. It was small consolation that the bombers were dead as well.

Véronique was scheduled for another surgery in two days, to continue to remove the shrapnel that was threatening her life. The risk of infection and septicemia from the filth with which the bomb was made was great. The apartment where they had been built had been discovered by then, and the bombs identified as triacetone triperoxide bombs, similar to those in the Paris attacks. The components were all items easily obtained in pharmacies and hardware stores.

Bernard went back to Paris on the train that night, with a heavy heart after what he'd been told. They had promised to call him as soon as they had further news. Once home, he called the hospital every few hours for news of Véronique. She was not expected to regain consciousness for several months, after many additional surgeries. After those to save her major organs, there would be the cosmetic ones. The doctor had said that it would be impossible to determine for some time the degree of visible damage to her face and body, but they expected it to be severe. It was possible that Véronique might be unrecognizable if she survived, even after reconstructive surgery. They had said that they would need photographs of her eventually, if she survived, to replicate her face as closely as they could. But he warned Bernard not to expect a miracle. She would look very different if she survived. Finding photographs of her was the one thing that would be easy. All they had to do was buy any magazine on the stands, and she would be in it. They didn't sound optimistic about the results they could achieve, given the extensive damage that she had sustained in the blast. She had been standing shockingly close to the bomb when it was detonated.

He lay awake all night and felt sick every time he thought of her. She was so young to be in such a dire situation with so much damage. He realized too that they had not made the connection to who she was, which was just as well. The last thing they needed was to have the press all over her, saying that her face had been destroyed. They had bigger problems on their hands without the press adding more drama for Véronique to have to cope with when she regained consciousness. He just prayed that she would. She was going to have so much to deal with, as well as the heartbreak of losing her mother. Bernard was the executor of Marie-Helene's estate, all of which had been left to the benefit of her daughter. Véronique would be well cared for forever, but what kind of life would she have now if her face was destroyed? She was such a young, beautiful girl. Véronique had lost her mother and her career in a single instant. Bernard couldn't imagine it, as he sat awake long into the night, with the tears sliding down his cheeks.

Chapter 3

The world was still reverberating with the attack on the Brussels airport when Véronique underwent her second surgery, and then her third and a fourth. She had held up so far, and after the third surgery, her internal organs were less compromised. The areas near her arteries had been cleared, her liver had suffered the greatest damage but could regenerate in time. The wounds on her body were deep, but she had lost no limbs, unlike many of the victims, both in Brussels and in Paris, who had lost arms and legs and hands and feet, either in the blast, or from gangrene in the days immediately after.

Marie-Helene's law partner continued to get daily reports, which were not encouraging. Marie-Helene's remains were in a military morgue in Brussels, with so many others waiting for instructions from the families. Bernard did not want to make any decisions about Marie-Helene's interment until Véronique was conscious and could make those decisions herself, if she was alive to do so. And if not, he would bury them together.

In June, three months almost to the day after the bomb explosion at Zaventem Airport, the surgeons at the military hospital made the decision to take Véronique out of the medically induced coma, take her off the respirator, and let her breathe on her own. She was very foggy at first, and didn't understand where she was or why she was there, and by the next day, she remembered the blast and where they had been going. She was still in ICU where she could be observed by a team of nurses, with immediate help available if she suffered an unexpected complication, which was still a possibility. She wasn't fully out of the woods yet, and wouldn't be for some time.

One of the nurses came to move her in her bed, and Véronique looked at her with wide eyes, her face still heavily bandaged. She looked like a mummy, with the bandages covering her head as well, and an eye patch over her injured eye. They had saved the eye in one of her many surgeries, but did not know yet if she would lose her sight in it.

"How's my mother?" she whispered to the nurse who was gently shifting her position. She had not been out of bed in three months, and was even thinner and light as a feather. The one eye she could see out of looked anxious, as the nurse said something reassuring, and called the doctor when she left Véronique's cubicle. This was the moment they had already discussed with a team of psychiatrists. A psychiatrist appeared in her room an hour later. She was a woman in her early fifties. She had a motherly style with her patients. They had been facing new challenges with more than a hundred civilian patients to deal with, which was very different from treating war-torn soldiers, injured in military action.

"How are you feeling, Véronique?" the psychiatrist asked her. She nodded and didn't answer. She hadn't talked in a long time, her voice was a croak when she tried to speak, and her throat still felt raw from the respirator. "Are you in pain?" the doctor asked her, and she shook her head. Her hands were bandaged too, from the wounds she had sustained on her hands and arms.

"How is my mother?" she asked again. It was the most pressing question on her mind. The doctor looked at her quietly, and as gently as possible explained that Marie-Helene had not survived the bomb. Véronique began gasping for air as soon as she said it. She couldn't breathe and couldn't speak. The psychiatrist stayed with her, speaking calmly to her for two hours, and they finally sedated her. It was a fact that had to be faced and they thought she was well enough to hear it now. But they had no way of knowing how close Véronique had been to her mother and all that she meant to her.

Bernard Aubert came from Paris the next day, and they cried together. Véronique couldn't believe what had happened. She was willing to have sustained all the damage she had, if only her mother were still alive. Véronique couldn't imagine her life without her. She was decimated by grief. She was able to speak in a stronger voice by the next day.

"And Cyril?" she asked Bernard, and he looked blank. "Cyril Buxton, he was with us. He's a friend of mine. He spent the night with us in Brussels, and he was flying back to London as soon as we took off. He was standing with us when it . . . happened." She faltered on the last word and couldn't make herself say the word "bomb."

"I don't know," he said. "I'll look into it. I didn't know anyone else was with you." He was surprised. After he left her, he checked the official list of casualties they had at the hospital, and found that Cyril was on it. When he inquired, he was told that like Véronique's mother, he had died in the initial explosion. His family had already claimed his remains. Bernard spent the night in Brussels, and told Véronique the next morning. She was shocked and saddened, and couldn't understand why she had survived and they hadn't. Bernard explained it as the hand of destiny, not having any better answer. She was deeply depressed about all of it, understandably, especially her mother, but she was sad about Cyril too. He was such a sweet, innocent, fun-loving boy, and didn't deserve to have his life cut short. None of them did, and she felt terrible for his parents, losing their only child.

"He was twenty-seven years old," she said to Bernard. He looked a dozen years older since his law partner had died. He brought up the painful subject of what to do with Marie-Helene's body. A decision had to be made. Sobbing, Véronique decided to have her cremated, and have the ashes sent to Paris. Bernard promised to keep them until Véronique came home, and they could make arrangements for a memorial service then. It made it all seem even more final. Véronique cried for hours after he left. She was crying for Cyril now too.

* * *

Two days later, Véronique was back in surgery, on her face this time, for the first of many reconstructive surgeries. Bernard had supplied the photographs they asked for. Marie-Helene's office was full of framed photographs of her beautiful daughter. He sent them directly to the plastic surgeon, who sat staring at them for a long time before the day of the surgery. He had been given an impossible task to restore Véronique to anything like she had looked before the explosion. There was no way he could even come close, and they had not yet told Véronique how extensive her injuries were, or how her face had been altered, and she couldn't see it under the heavy bandages.

He had made meticulous drawings and diagrams of what he had to repair and how to go about it, and he stood studying her carefully for a long time, as she lay on the operating table, once she'd been anesthetized. The surgeon assisting him looked at her too, and the two physicians exchanged a long glance.

"It would be a fascinating challenge if it weren't so tragic," the senior surgeon said quietly to his colleague. "It's as though someone drew a line down the center of her face, destroyed one half, and left the other intact." The wounds on one side had been superficial, and had healed in the past three months under the bandages. The other half was unrecognizable for the moment, but even once it was repaired, the surgeon recognized that there would be two or possibly three deep scars intersecting her face. There would be no way to remove them entirely. He studied her photographs again, and began the surgery. It was painstaking minute work, and he was satisfied after eight hours in surgery that they had done as much as they could for the moment. They bandaged her face again, and she was moved to the recovery room, as the assisting surgeon stayed to talk to him.

"What do you think?" he asked him. The chief surgeon was one of their best and had performed some near miracles in the past, but he wasn't a magician.

"We can only do what we can. I'm going to try everything we're able to do, but it would take a miracle. The scars are too deep." Half her face had been destroyed by shrapnel. "I don't know how the other side remained so untouched. It must have been the angle at which she was standing when it happened, or some odd quirk of fate."

"You know who she is, don't you?" his colleague asked and the chief surgeon nodded.

"I didn't at first, but I realized when I saw the photographs they sent me, and I did some research. She's one of the biggest models in the world, or she was until now. She's incredibly beautiful. It really is unbelievably cruel to see what happened."

"When are you going to tell her?" he asked him.

"When I have to, and when we've done some more repair work on the worst of it. She knows there was damage to her face. She just doesn't know how long-term it is. She hasn't asked much about it, but she hasn't been awake for long, and she's been more concerned about her mother, who died when it happened. But eventually, this is going to be a big issue for her. Her modeling days are over. And if that was integral to her identity, and I assume it must have been, we're going to have a big problem. It's a very big deal to be an extraordinary beauty at one moment, and then sustain this kind of damage. Her whole self-image will be shattered, who she is, what she does, how she sees herself, how others see her, her whole career. This will be an enormous crisis for her. She'll have to rebuild her whole personality and identification system, not just her face."

"Do you know anything else about her?" the assistant surgeon asked him. They were up against a huge challenge, and were still talking about it as they left the operating room. They both felt drained after eight hours of surgery, and they felt great compassion for her, especially at her age, and seemingly with no one to support her.

"Very little," the chief surgeon answered. "The only contact is her mother's legal partner, and he hasn't told me much about her, other than that she has no relatives. He sent the photographs, and no further information. The photographs speak for themselves. She's an incredible beauty, and one of the biggest models in the world. What else is there to say?"

"It would help to know something about her character, how strong she is."

"She just lost her mother. That will be hard enough. And apparently there was a friend with them, who died too. Now her whole identity is altered."

"But at least she's alive," the assistant reminded him.

"Sometimes that's not enough. I don't consider myself a vain man, but I'm not sure how well I'd do if I lost half my face."

"The structure is still there. It's all the soft tissue that's the problem. At least the bone structure of her face is reparable."

"It's the rest I'm worried about, and she will be too. It will take a lot of guts to deal with something like this." They were both still troubled by it when they left each other after the surgery, and the head surgeon took the before and after photographs home with him that night to study them some more and try to decide what to repair in the next surgery. They had a long road ahead of them, and so did she. And she had the trauma to deal with as well.

Véronique asked very few questions after the surgery. And Dr. Moreau, the chief surgeon, wondered if she was afraid to. It was as though her mind didn't want to go there, and he decided that maybe it was just as well for now, but she couldn't hide from it forever. One day she would be back in a world full of mirrors, and would have to deal with people's reactions to how she looked. On the other hand, they had seen patients who had lost all four limbs, which might be even harder. She would be able to lead a normal life, she just wouldn't look the way she looked before, but that was huge, particularly after all the adulation of being a model. Her beauty had been a given before, and now it had been stolen from her.

The whole team was aware of what she would be facing, and they got a taste of the reality that would confront her once she left the hospital. There was no way of knowing who did it, but in July a story ran in a minor British tabloid saying that her face had been destroyed in the attack, and her career was over. Miraculously, no one else picked it up or believed it. Like saying she had an affair with an alien. The tabloid that ran it was known for its lack of credibility and untruths. But it was also obvious that someone at the hospital had been paid for the story. No one outside the hospital knew about her face. Bernard was furious about it, and the head of the hospital apologized and promised to be more vigilant. At Bernard's request, she never saw it. She was cut off from the world without a computer, and wasn't reading the newspapers, magazines, or even watching TV. But it gave the whole medical team a foretaste of what would happen when she went back to Paris, paparazzi chasing her, ordinary people taking photographs of her with their cellphones. Overnight, she would become a freak, and a victim of people's curiosity and baser instincts. Véronique didn't even have a cellphone at the hospital and didn't want one. Hers had disappeared in the explosion. She was still too sick to care, and she said that without her mother, there was no one she wanted to call. She didn't need to call her agent, since she couldn't work, and Bernard had notified them she'd be off for a while, without further explanation. She was also in deep mourning for her mother, so she didn't want to talk to friends and other models. She had nothing to say. Her grief was all encompassing, and with no contact with the world, she was safe for now, but it wouldn't last. Her half-damaged face would identify her as a victim forever. They were going to suggest to her that she wear a surgical mask when she went home and use it whenever she went out, at least until the surgeries on her face were complete, and maybe even forever if she couldn't deal with the inevitable stares and comments.

Véronique never saw the second-rate British tabloid magazine with her photo on the cover. The photograph had been torn in half lengthwise, so all she had was half a face, and inside the magazine was the whole story of the explosion, and that she'd been in it. Véronique would have hated the story, it made her an object of pity, but fortunately she never knew about it and was spared the humiliation of public exposure. The day would come when she'd have to know the truth, that half her face had been ruined, and the other half was a cruel reminder of what it once had been.

The summer went by slowly and painfully for her. Doctors and nurses came and went on vacation. She was still in the hospital, with assorted aches and pains resulting from her wounds. And she had another operation every two weeks. She'd have four more by the end of the summer. The plastic surgeon wasn't satisfied with the results, and she healed slowly, which made it harder to see progress. Her face had improved slightly, but not enough. She still hadn't seen it yet herself, and had no idea how far they'd come. The bone structure in her face was aligned again, but much of the tissue over it was deeply damaged.

She had no distractions, and couldn't read easily with the injury to her eye. Her good eye functioned but tired quickly.

She thought about her mother all summer, and the positive things she would have said to get her through a terrible experience like this.

She was thinking about that when Bernard came to see her one day. He was leaving the next day for his summer vacation, which he spent in Brittany every year. He felt that it was time to share her mother's will with her, and there were things she needed to know about Marie-Helene's estate. He had warned her that he was going to bring it with him. She was dreading it, it made her mother's death all the more real. Véronique thought about it every day anyway, and about Cyril, and the horrifying circumstances in which they'd died. She wanted to write to his parents, but hadn't been able to make herself do it yet. Since he was an only child, she could just imagine how hard it had hit his parents. She wondered if they blamed her because she had been with him at the time. She felt guilty herself because she was alive and he wasn't. Although being alive was a question of degree at the moment. She still felt dead inside, and at times she wished that she had died too in the explosion.

The psychiatrist came to see her almost every day to talk about it. She felt like a prisoner now. All the medical staff was leaving on summer vacation, like the rest of Europe, and she was still in the hospital enduring surgery after surgery. The terrorists had committed the crime, and she and the other victims were being punished for it. She wanted to go home, but she was afraid to, and she knew it would break her heart to walk into her mother's apartment and find her not there, in the home where Véronique had grown up. In her fantasies sometimes, she told herself that her mother was in Paris, and she would see her when she went home, and then the truth would come crashing down on her like the airport roof caving in on her again. It was becoming harder and harder to escape the truth.

When Bernard came to see her, he was carrying a very large manila envelope, and he spread the contents out on Véronique's hospital bed. She had been moved to her own room by then, and was no longer in ICU. It was actually lonelier being in a single room. She didn't see all the activity of the intensive care ward and the people in it, and lay lost in her own thoughts most of the time. The psychiatrist thought she needed quiet time to process what she had to deal with. She believed that she still needed reconstructive surgery on her face, but she didn't yet know that little could be done to restore her. She no longer had the strong support of her mother, nor the distraction of the successful career she was used to. Everything in her life had changed, more than she even knew.

Bernard had brought a copy of her mother's will, which was not surprising. She left everything to Véronique, including her apartment in the seventeenth, which was Véronique's now. It was not luxurious, but it represented a solid investment, and a tangible asset with some value. She had few other possessions, but he had brought her bank statements as well, which were a big surprise to Véronique, and had been to Bernard too. There was a bank account, which a cover letter in the will explained had been left to Véronique by her father, for her support and education well into the future. And instead of using it for that purpose, Marie-Helene had preserved all of it, invested it wisely, and supported Véronique herself from what she earned in her successful law practice. Véronique's father had left her a million dollars, which astounded her. Marie-Helene had less than that put aside herself from her earnings over the years, and the value of the apartment. And in a separate account, Marie-Helene had put the money that Véronique had earned as a model, right from the beginning, which was just over two million dollars. She had invested that well too, and it had grown considerably. So between her father, her mother, and the money she had earned herself, she had well over three million dollars, closer to four, as well as her mother's apartment. And she had her own apartment to sell too. She didn't need two apartments. Selling her mother's apartment seemed like a sacrilege, and she wouldn't do it. She had decided to move back in, and sell her own small apartment in the seventh. She had more than enough money to live well on. Thanks to her father, her mother's careful management, and her own hard work, she was very well set, and what her mother had left her in money and real estate was icing on the cake.

There was a large manila envelope of photographs of Marie-Helene with Véronique's father, and a number of him holding Véronique when she was a baby. There were many framed at the apartment, but dozens more in the envelope, with Marie-Helene beaming beside him, which Véronique was happy to have, as an illustration of her history, and tangible proof that she had had a father. She looked very much like him, which Marie-Helene always said. And the money she had left in various guises was a real windfall. His name was Bill Smith, and she felt like such an orphan now, she wondered if she should change her last name to Véronique Vincent-Smith, to honor both her late mother and her father. It was something to think about.

Other than the financial statements, which were very neat and well organized, there was a letter in a sealed envelope. Reading it would be like getting a message from her mother from the grave. It seemed morbid and intimidating, and yet she was hungry to read it, and hear from her mother one last time. She wondered when she had written it and what it would say. Her mother had no deep secrets to reveal that she knew of. She led a quiet, transparent life, so Véronique assumed that it was just a tender goodbye, written long in advance, perhaps at an emotional moment. It would be hard to read but she was eager for it, and decided to read it after Bernard left, so she could savor it when she was alone, and cry if she needed to. She put the sealed envelope on the table next to her hospital bed, to read when he was gone. She put the rest back in the envelope, thanked Bernard for bringing it, and slipped it into a drawer in the night table so it was near at hand.

He stayed for another hour, chatting with her, and it was nice to have company. He was her only visitor. She wished him a good vacation when he finally stood up to go. She lay quietly in bed for a long time afterward, trying to get up the courage to open her mother's letter. She couldn't imagine what was in it. She missed her mother more than ever. It was a physical pain that never left her, worse than her wounds from the shrapnel.

Chapter 4

Véronique saw as soon as she opened her mother's letter that it had been written a year before, on her twenty-first birthday. In her mother's neat, careful hand, she had said that now that Véronique was an adult, she felt she owed it to Véronique to tell her the truth about her father. And she planned to do so, at an appropriate time, or after her death, if she hadn't told her yet, which was the case, as it turned out. A shiver ran up her spine as she read the words. The Truth About Her Father. What truth was there to know, other than what her mother had already told her? She reiterated what Véronique already knew, that he was American, and an attorney. He had been sixty-one when she was born, the same year he died, and they hadn't been married. But in the letter, her mother stunned her with two important details. The reason they hadn't married was that he already was, to someone else, with three children from that marriage. He had wanted to divorce his wife for years, and especially once he met Marie-Helene, but he had had powerful political aspirations, possibly even a shot at the presidency. In fact, Marie-Helene explained, he had run as a vice presidential candidate, lost the election with his running mate, and had subsequently become a senator. But a scandal, having an affair as a married man, with a love child and a mistress in France, would have ruined him if it had come out, and destroyed his dreams of politics forever. He had spent a considerable amount of time with Marie-Helene in France, and loved it there. And he had been present at Véronique's birth and stayed for a month after. But in the end, Marie-Helene confessed in the letter that she had stepped aside so as not to stand in his way, and hurt his chances politically. She had ended their relationship so he could pursue his dreams. What shocked Véronique was that he had let her.

The letter went on to say that he had provided a large amount of money for Véronique's future, to ensure her safety, education, and comfort. He and Marie-Helene had only seen each other once after that, in a secret meeting, but remained in occasional contact. She assumed that Véronique knew about the money by then, since her instructions to Bernard as her executor were that neither the money nor the letter was to be revealed to Véronique until after her mother's death, just as he had done. He had no knowledge of the contents of the letter, only the financial arrangements, as executor.

The shocker was that Bill had not died when Véronique was an infant. Marie-Helene had left him, for his sake, and had made the ultimate sacrifice herself, of her own happiness and well-being to honor his political dreams. It struck Véronique that he must have been a selfish man to let her mother do that, and heartless to leave them both. The money he had left their daughter was the reward for Marie-Helene's being entirely selfless. They had agreed to tell Véronique that he had died, when during all this time, he was very much alive. Véronique didn't know if he still was. Given his age at her birth, he would be eighty-three now, but he had been alive when Marie-Helene wrote the letter a year earlier. He was still a senator at the time, although she knew he suffered from ill health, and was planning to retire. His real name was William Hayes, and he had never tried to see his daughter, although Marie-Helene said he inquired about her from time to time, and never lost touch.

As soon as Véronique read his name, it sounded familiar to her, and she realized why he also looked familiar in the photographs. She had seen pictures of him somewhere, maybe in the press. So he had had the successful political career he wanted so badly, and Marie-Helene had lost the man she loved, and Véronique a father. She didn't like the fact that her mother had been deceptive about it, but it was hard to be angry at her now that she was gone. She had sacrificed so much for his well-being, because she loved him. If anything, Véronique was more touched than angry, and had never lacked for anything, thanks to her mother. The money he had left her had been untouched, to be used later on. He had given it to Marie-Helene when they parted, so that it didn't become entangled in a legal battle at his death, and by giving it early he had spared everyone embarrassment. Marie-Helene said that his wife had never known about her. It explained why they had never married, and she affirmed that he had been the love of her life. Véronique thought she had paid a high price for it, and there were tears running down her cheeks as she read the letter. More than anything, she felt sorry for her mother, who had given up so much. And she had been such a devoted, loving mother.

The letter created a dilemma for Véronique. She was no longer an orphan now, as she had thought. She had lost her mother, but her father was alive. The temptation was great to try and see him, so that she had a connection with someone in the world, and wasn't entirely alone. She hated what he had done to her mother and how selfish he had been, but he was still her father and she was curious about him. She had no idea how to reach out to him, and wanted to think about it. She was grateful her mother had written the letter, and realized it must have been painful for her. She apologized to Véronique for lying to her, but Véronique was mature enough to understand and forgive her for it. The one she had more trouble forgiving was her father for letting her mother slip away, and abandoning them both. She thought he had a right to know that her mother had died, which seemed like another valid reason to contact him. She was sorely tempted to do so. She wondered if he'd even respond. It gave her something to think about, other than her injuries, and her own uncertain future. The only gift after all her losses was knowing that she had a father and he was alive.

She read the letter several times again that night, and looked at the photographs of Bill Hayes and her mother. Her parents. She wondered what kind of man he was, cheating on his wife with a mistress, and having a child with her, and then abandoning them in favor of his political career. If nothing else, he sounded very selfish. She spent the rest of July and all of August thinking about it between her surgeries. She was due to be released in September. If her father had health problems, she wanted to meet him before he died. She had a lot to think about now that she knew about him and she was grateful for her mother's letter and the truth at last.

Things seemed very slow at the hospital in July and August, with many of the doctors away for their summer holidays. She had two more surgeries to remove more shrapnel in July, and another long plastic surgery on her face and a shorter one in August. She had been in the hospital for five months by then, and had improved enough to start feeling restless and cooped up. She still had odd, inexplicable aches and pains from the shrapnel throughout her body, and was told she'd have to live with it. She could see shapes and light and dark with her injured eye now, which they said might not improve. Technically, she could drive with an eye patch, but she didn't feel safe driving with impaired vision, whether legal or not. She still needed another surgery in a few months, but the ones in August were the last ones for now. She wondered how long it would take so one couldn't see the scars. She knew that plastic surgeons could perform miracles.

When the bandages came off in early September, she got her first glimpse of the truth. She had two deep scars that ran across the right side of her face, and a third smaller one below it. They said there would be some improvement, and they would pale, but they couldn't be fully erased. She just stared at them in the mirror and cried. Half her face was untouched and the other half badly scarred.

The reality was shocking when she saw it. She almost fainted when she first saw the injured side in contrast to the unscarred half of her face. It looked like a bad before and after photo. She realized then that this was her face now. Half perfect and half damaged, like a terrible curse someone had put on her. The psychiatrist spent hours with her while she cried. She tried walking around the hospital in the surgical mask they gave her to conceal her scars and felt smothered and like an invalid.

When she got back to her room, she stood in front of the mirror again, crying, and refused to talk to the psychiatrist the next day. She was tired of all the doctors and nurses, the bandages, the smell of the hospital, the pain after each surgery, and the terrifying sight her face had become. How could she see anyone or leave her house? She would have to wear the face mask forever. The surgeon said the scar would become less vivid in a few months and the smaller scars would disappear, but the three deepest ones could not be repaired more than they were.

She had disappeared from her life after the explosion and had seen no one except Bernard Aubert. But how would she go back now? And she didn't have her mother to lean on. She wanted to run away and hide. But wherever she went, her half-ruined face would be with her. She couldn't imagine facing anyone with it, or leading a normal life again. Not only was her career over, but all semblance of a life.

She was sitting in her room, contemplating her future, and the prospect seemed grim, when the phone rang. She assumed it was Bernard, since he was the only one who called her. No further information had been given to her modeling agency, other than that she had been at the Brussels airport and couldn't work for several months. And there was no work anyway in the summer, so they hadn't called. She had turned off the phone in her hospital room and hardly turned it on in five months. Many people had written to her about her mother, and she hadn't had the energy yet to answer them, although she'd been touched by their messages when Bernard forwarded them to her. Many of them were unaware that Véronique had been injured, and she had no desire to explain it to them, especially now. Bernard's secretary picked up the mail at the apartment every week, paid the bills, and sent the rest to her.

She picked up the phone in her room, expecting to hear Bernard's voice, and instead a young female voice said a cautious hello.

"Véro, is that you?" It took her a minute to place it and then realized it was Gabriella Foch, a girl she had gone to school with, who had moved to Brussels with her parents five years before. She was startled to hear her voice.

"Gabriella?"

"Yes. I was just reading in a Belgian magazine about the attack on Zaventem, and I saw your picture. There was a whole page of little photos the size of postage stamps of all the victims, and there was one of you, and I read your name. I couldn't believe it. I'm so sorry about your mom." They hadn't been close, but had been in the same class for years and she was a nice girl. "It said that all the victims were taken to the military hospital. I thought I'd just try to see if you were still here. It said that many people are. Are you okay?" Véronique paused, not sure what to answer. Something polite or the truth?

"Yes, I'm okay. I'm going home in two weeks." She didn't say that she'd had twenty-six surgeries and half her face had been destroyed, and there would be shrapnel in her body forever. But others were worse off, without limbs, and she was alive. The psychiatrists kept stressing that, but she wasn't sure now if having survived was a blessing or a curse.

"Can I come and see you?"

"It's pretty depressing here," Véronique said glumly, not sure if she wanted to see her or not. She'd have to wear the mask. But maybe how Gabriella would react would be a good test of what lay ahead.

"I don't care if it's depressing. I want to see you. I wish I'd known sooner. I've been following you since we moved here. I hated it here at first, but I like it now. I'm working for my father in his art gallery. Will you go back to modeling now when you go home?"

"I . . . uh . . . I don't think so. It's too soon." She didn't know what else to say, and Gabriella was afraid to ask her what injuries had kept her in the hospital for five months. She hoped she hadn't lost a leg or an arm. The article she'd read said many had, and the bombs had been specially built to do as much damage as possible to human bodies. The same had been true about the attacks in France.

"Can I come?" She sounded excited about seeing her old class-mate. Véronique agreed to see her the following afternoon, and re-gretted it as soon as she hung up. She wanted to cancel immediately, but forced herself to stick to the plan. She hadn't talked to anyone her own age, or seen a friend, in five months. She didn't want to see any of her modeling friends in Paris. How could she now with the face she was going home with? She had no idea who she was any-more. Everything that defined her had been destroyed. She didn't feel like a person anymore, or a woman, or even a girl. She was a member of the walking wounded, someone to pity or to look away from in horror.

She was wearing a hospital dressing gown and pajamas at the appointed time the next day. She hadn't worn normal clothes since she'd been admitted. Hers had been torn to shreds in the explosion, and no one had replaced them. She didn't need clothes anyway. She couldn't go anywhere. But she realized that she'd need something to wear when she went home. She put the surgical mask in place just before Gabriella came. She brushed her hair back in a ponytail, and the cruel irony was that when she turned her face one way, she looked like herself, and if she turned in the opposite direction, the full horror of her injuries were all one saw. The damage was completely contained on the right side of her face. She adjusted the surgical mask again as she heard a knock on the door, and Gabriella walked in, looked as she had in school, barely older, in a pretty navy blue summer dress with a white collar. She smiled as soon as she saw Véronique and walked toward her.

"Can I hug you? Will I hurt anything?" she asked her, and Véronique smiled.

"No, I'm fine. I'm full of shrapnel still, but it's better and hugging won't hurt me." Gabriella hugged her gingerly as Véronique realized that no one had hugged her or touched her affectionately in five months. The tenderness of it brought tears to her eyes. She saw then that Gabbie had brought her a small bouquet of pink roses.

53

They sat down in the room's only two chairs. "Do you want to go out to the garden?" she offered.

"Whatever you want," Gabriella said gently. She thought her old friend's eyes looked tired and sad. "Do you have to wear the mask?"

"It's so I don't get exposed to infection," she said, looking distracted. Gabriella could only imagine what she'd been through, after reading the article about the explosion and the havoc it wrought on the victims.

"The whole thing is so awful. It makes you afraid to go anywhere. I knew two people at the metro station, but they managed to come out unharmed. I had a friend at the Bataclan in Paris in November. He lost an arm, but at least he survived." She guessed that all of Véronique's injuries must have been internal since she didn't appear to be missing any limbs, but she could see scars on her arms from the hundreds of lacerations she'd had from the flying bits of metal and glass. It looked to her like Véronique had been lucky.

They took a walk in the garden, sat in the shade for a while, and walked back to Véronique's room. It was a nice visit and Véronique enjoyed it, although it was odd talking to her through the mask. She felt smothered by it, and dishonest somehow, as though she was pretending to be someone else now, the old Véronique instead of the one she had become. She hated the pretense of it, as though she still looked like she used to. But in fact, nothing was the same now. She felt like a different person.

"I feel stupid wearing the mask," she said in a soft voice to Gabriella.

"If it's dangerous for you to be exposed to people's germs, then you're smart to wear it. You don't want to get sick now."

"It's not that . . . and I'm not sick." With a trembling hand and a simple gesture, she unhooked the paper mask from her right ear, and took it off, as Gabriella stared at her, with a full view of both halves of her face, the old and the new. Her eyes grew wide as she saw the scars on the right side, burst into tears, and couldn't stop crying. What she saw was so devastating and so upsetting, she had been totally unprepared for what Véronique had gone through and the damage the bomb had done.

"Oh, Véro, I'm so sorry. . . . Oh my God, how could they do that to you?" Véronique was crying too, and they sat talking and holding hands, but Gabriella's reaction was what she had needed to know. How could she possibly let anyone see the face she had now? The answer was that she couldn't. No one would be able to tolerate it.

"I suppose I was lucky. Some people lost arms and legs, or both. It's only my face." She tried to minimize it in her own mind too, but she couldn't. The challenge she was facing was huge, and Gabriella had confirmed it.

"You were so beautiful," she said almost enviously, and then caught herself. "You still are. Will it get better?" she asked in a hushed voice.

"A little, not much. They can do more surgeries to smooth down the scars, but they said they won't go away completely. The scars are too deep. They want to let it heal for a few months. I might see a doctor in Paris. But they've done all they can for now. They told me to wear the mask, but I hate it. You're the only person I've seen till now, except for the doctors and nurses and my mother's law partner, but he didn't see me without the bandages. If I don't wear the mask, I'll frighten children on the street," Véronique said sadly.

"No, you won't. I just wasn't prepared when you took it off. I was guessing that all your injuries were internal since I didn't see any missing limbs."

"It sliced a piece off my liver, but apparently that grows back," Véronique said. "I'll just have to get used to it. It's kind of hideously ironic, since I've made a living from being 'beautiful' for four years. So I'm out of work now too."

"What will you do?" Gabriella asked, worried for her. There were girls she knew who would have committed suicide with a face as badly scarred as Véronique's. She hoped Véronique wouldn't be one of them, but she had never been particularly vain in school. She was just incredibly beautiful. This was going to be a huge change for her, and a lot to deal with.

"I thought of wearing a burqa, but I'd feel stupid and dishonest doing that too. I guess it's the surgical mask or nothing. I think people will be afraid to hire me for a normal job, I'd frighten the clients." She felt like a leper and a pariah as she said it, but Gabriella knew it was true. "And I don't know how to do anything except pose for the camera."

"Maybe you could be a photographer," Gabriella suggested.

"Maybe. I hadn't thought of it. I've just been kind of surviving from day to day between surgeries. I haven't thought past this, until now. And it will be so weird going home to an empty house without my mother. I'm going to move into her apartment." It would be like crawling back into the womb for her, which she needed now, but painful without Marie-Helene providing the womb.

"Stay in touch, Véro," Gabriella said when she left. "I never get to Paris anymore, but if I do, I'll call. And you can always call me if you need to talk. You must have a million friends." She had followed her old classmate's jet-set life for years, and they were light-years apart now.

"I don't know. I'm not friendly with that many models. I was working all the time. The boy I was dating was with us, just by a weird coincidence. He was killed too." Mentioning him reminded Véronique of something she wanted to do, and hadn't been able to face yet. Gabriella had opened a door that afternoon, and Véronique realized that she couldn't hide from the real world forever.

Gabriella stood up to go, and Véronique walked her to the door without her mask. They hugged again at the door, and she thanked Gabriella for the visit and the flowers, and Gabriella turned in the doorway.

"I'm sorry I reacted the way I did when I saw your face. I was so sorry for you. I'm just glad you're alive. That's all that matters."

"Is it? I keep asking myself that. What matters now? How I look or what I do or who I am? I'm not sure who I am anymore. I'm not the same person I was six months ago, inside or out."

"No one would be," Gabriella said. "You'll figure it out." But they both knew it wouldn't be easy. Finding herself now and a new path in life would be harder than twenty-six surgeries and surviving the bomb. She had to find her way now, and she had no idea how to do it. Gabriella's reaction to seeing her scarred face had told her all she needed to know about how people would react to her. One thing was sure. She wasn't beautiful anymore. That was all she had been before. Now she would have to be more. But what? And how? She had absolutely no idea.

Chapter 5

After Gabriella's visit, Véronique asked the nurse for some paper and an envelope. She had a letter to write that was long over-due. Gabriella had been an emissary from a broader world, beyond the hospital, surgeries, and medications. Véronique was going home soon, and beginning to think about the world she had left behind and almost forgotten for the past nearly six months. Cyril had been part of that forgotten life, although she hadn't forgotten him.

She wrote a letter to his mother that night, and couldn't stop cry-ing while she wrote it. There was so much to say, but she didn't know his parents well, and had only met them once. As an only child, she could only imagine how immense their loss was. She told his mother how sorry she was, and what a lovely young man he had been. She offered them heartfelt sympathy and apologized for not writing to them sooner. She said only that it had been a difficult time for her, and didn't offer twenty-six surgeries as a valid excuse. At least she was still alive, but he wasn't.

She didn't expect a response, but she felt relieved after she wrote it, sealed the envelope, and asked the nurse if she would mail it for her. She remembered his address by heart, and felt a wave of survivor guilt wash over her again that night. He had only gone to the check-in counter with her to help her and her mother, and had been there at just the wrong moment, as they all were. He had been standing next to her mother, helping her with her bag, while Véronique was only a few feet away, the few feet that had made a life and death difference. She had no idea why she had survived and they hadn't, other than the random hand of fate.

The next morning, Véronique took another step into real life. Bernard had left her some cash in case she needed it, which she hadn't so far. She asked one of the younger nurses to buy some clothes for her, some jeans and a sweater and a pair of sneakers. She had no clothes to go home in. She asked for a bag for her toiletries, and a purse of some kind. She hadn't thought about clothes to wear for months, and lived in hospital gowns and pajamas, with paper slippers.

At Véronique's request, Bernard had had her mother's secretary empty her apartment in the seventh, put the furniture in storage, and send everything else in boxes to her mother's apartment. Her apartment was for sale, and everything she owned was now at her mother's. She would have to go through all of it, and her mother's clothes and papers, when she went home. At least it would give her something to do for a while.

Dr. Verbier, her main psychiatrist, questioned her about it that afternoon. With her release from the hospital weeks away, the sessions had gotten more intense, about her plans. Who she was going to see, where she would live, if she had contacted any friends, how she was going to occupy her time.

"How do you feel about going to live in your mother's apartment?" the doctor asked her.

"It's what I want to do," Véronique said quietly. She didn't want to have to justify it. "I grew up there. I'm selling my apartment, it's on the market now." She wasn't attached to it and had no need for it anymore.

"It will be hard for you, Véronique, being in the place where your mother lived, without her now."

"I own the apartment," Véronique said, eager to get off the subject.

"It will be filled with memories, and all of her belongings." She knew it would be hard, but it would be comforting too. A part of her fantasized that her mother would be there when she got home. It was still hard to believe that she wouldn't be.

She still had her mother's memorial service and burial to arrange. Bernard was keeping her mother's ashes for her, in the office safe.

"Have you thought about what you're going to do when you get home, for work?" Dr. Verbier asked her. She was embarrassed to admit that, thanks to her mother and her own earnings set aside, she had the luxury of not working for a while. The doctor was well aware that she had been a highly successful model, and would have to choose a new career now. Véronique had nothing but change to adjust to when she got home. No part of her previous life was still intact. All of the psychiatric staff had discussed her case, and were concerned that she could be a suicide risk, but Dr. Verbier was fairly sure she wasn't. But there was no question in her mind, Véronique's re-entry after the hospital would be a tremendous adjustment, and she was liable to have a hard time with it. She had to find a whole new direction for her life. Véronique was tired of talking to them about it. She felt ready to go home, no matter how challenging it was.

She had another project she wanted to pursue, and asked Bernard to send her a laptop so she could start even before she left the hospital. She started working on it as soon as the laptop arrived. She wanted to research her father, and read everything about him. She wanted to see what kind of man he was.

She found all the information about him that she wanted, and discovered that he had retired in June, shortly after he lost his wife. Marie-Helene had died in March, and Florence Hayes a month later. Bill Hayes was retired now. He had given up his Senate seat due to ill health, one report said.

She read everything she could about him, from his voting record to the failed presidential campaign many years earlier when he had been the vice presidential candidate. She thought about how strange it would have been if her father had been the president of the United States. But his political ambitions seemed to have cooled a little after they lost the election. He won his Senate seat then, and had had a highly respected career. She couldn't help wondering if he had ever regretted letting Marie-Helene get away, if his senatorial career had been worth losing the woman he loved, and who had loved him so deeply.

He looked handsome in the photographs she saw on the Internet. There were several of them with his wife and children during his campaigns, and she felt sorry for her mother again when she saw them. She wondered if her mother had followed him online, or if it would have been too painful to do so. She wasn't a woman who cried about the past. She had always been energetic, optimistic, and forward thinking, and had never expressed any regrets to her daughter, even in her final letter.

Véronique spent hours reading about her father, and found a mailing address for him in New York. She had no idea if he would ever see the letter if she wrote to him, but she wanted to try. She spent two days composing the letter, determined not to be indiscreet or to cause any problems. She addressed him as Senator Hayes, and regretfully informed him that Marie-Helene Vincent had passed away in the bombing of the Brussels airport. She introduced herself as Marie-Helene's daughter, and respectfully asked if a conversation with him would be possible, by email or by phone, and supplied her email address and her mother's home phone number, which she assumed he knew anyway, since Marie-Helene had already been living there when they met, and they had been in contact from time to time in the years since, according to the letter she had left.

Véronique read the letter several times, combing it for any overly personal references, or anything he might find offensive. It was a letter that even a secretary could have read. She wondered if he'd ever see it, or if he would welcome contact with her, but she knew she had to try, for her own sake and her mother's. Her mother had finally disclosed who her father was, and Véronique had the feeling that she had opened that door so that Véronique could contact him if she wished, once her mother was gone. She sealed the letter carefully, and asked one of the nurses to mail it for her. She had included the date that she would be returning to Paris, and said that she had been at the airport with her mother, without providing any details of the injuries she had sustained herself. She didn't want his pity, but she wanted a better sense of who he was. Her mother had referred to him as remarkable and extraordinary and said he was a wonderful man. Véronique wanted to know if it was true, and how he could have left them out of his life for so long. She guessed that his three children were at least twenty years older than she was, and she could easily have been his grandchild when she was born, and he could have been her mother's father.

She spent her final days in the hospital doing practical things to prepare for when she got home. She bought a cellphone and reactivated her old number. She turned it on a few times, but there were no messages and it never rang. Since she was no longer modeling or active at her agency, it appeared as though everyone had forgotten her, which seemed just as well now. There was no longer any question of her modeling again. She was one of those tragic stories people would tell one day of the supermodel who had been blown up in a terrorist attack and never returned. The photographs of her would surface again now and then, as one of the biggest models of her day, with a brief career that lasted only a few years.

She wore the surgical mask when she went to buy her cellphone, and the salesman looked at her questioningly but didn't comment. She felt like one of those neurotic women who were germophobes, but better that than the truth, that half of her face looked like something out of a horror movie. The doctors assured her that the brightness of the worst scars on her face would fade somewhat with time, but for the moment, after her most recent surgery, the scars were still very vivid. She tried not to look at herself in the mirror when she brushed her teeth or combed her hair, but her eyes always traveled there and she stared at her face, as though hoping that by magic it would have radically improved, or the scars be gone. She still found it hard to believe that she would look like that forever, but it was equally hard to believe that she would never see her mother again.

Bernard called a few days before she was due to leave the hospital, to make sure she was all right, and ask how she was getting home. He had offered to accompany her, although she knew he was very busy, and she had told him she preferred to make the trip alone.

Two days before she left, she had an answer from Cyril's mother. It was measured and polite, and expressed her condolences for the loss of Véronique's mother, but the letter wasn't warm. Reading between the lines, she had the feeling that Lady Buxton blamed her for Cyril's untimely death. If he hadn't been with her, he wouldn't have been in Brussels or anywhere near the attack. She said that his death had been a terrible shock for them, and an immeasurable loss. She expressed the hope that Véronique had recovered from her injuries. Everything about the letter was an example of good manners and good breeding, but there was nothing affectionate or even barely compassionate in it for the last woman in their son's life. She was sure that his mother had asked herself the same question she had asked herself a thousand times. Why had she survived and he hadn't? He didn't deserve to die any more than any of the others, nor did she deserve the appalling injuries she had sustained. She had been to hell and back in the last six months, and still had a long way to go to recover from the trauma.

All of her psychiatrists had reservations about her going home, particularly with no one to go home to, and no family to support her through the inevitable difficulties she would face. But medically there was no longer any reason to keep her in the hospital, which was depressing for her too. Their overall decision was that she needed to get back into a more active life, to the degree she was able. She would have to return for further surgeries to effect some slight improvement to the scars on her face. There was still the potential risk that the shifting of any of the shrapnel still in her body could cause a life-threatening situation, but there was no way to predict that. They had done very little cosmetic work on the extensive scarring on her body, but Véronique had opted not to. She could always deal with that later, if she wanted to. The wounds were still very fresh. For now, she preferred to wear long-sleeve shirts and sweaters and trousers to conceal the scars on her body, rather than undergo additional surgeries. She said it didn't matter to her. She wasn't modeling anymore, and beauty was no longer a professional necessity, or of importance to her. The only scars that mattered to her were those on her face, so that she wouldn't be so shockingly disfigured, but they were the ones they were the least able to improve. They had done their very best, but even they were disappointed by the results. The unmarked half of her face served as a cruel reminder to them as well as Véronique of how perfect and flawless her face had been before.

She made a point of visiting the other victims she had met in the hospital before she left, although she hadn't gotten to know many of them very well. Most of them were too ill and damaged to leave their rooms, even six months after the explosion. She saw some of them occasionally in wheelchairs in the garden, missing limbs and accompanied by nurses. And for many months she hadn't been well enough to leave her room either, after her constant surgeries.

They wished her luck when she said goodbye to them. She gave a box of chocolates to the young woman in the room next to her, who had lost both arms and a foot, and had three young children who were being cared for by her mother, waiting for her at home. Her husband had died in the blast of the bomb. It reminded Véronique again that in many ways, she had been lucky. And even without working, she was financially able to take care of herself. Many of the victims were in dire financial straits since they weren't able to work, and government payments for the wounded had not kicked in yet. Victims of the attack in Paris four months earlier than the one in Brussels were still waiting for government funds too. The machinery of government did not move quickly. In many ways, Véronique was better off than her fellow victims.

The nurses gave her a cake and a little party the night before she left, and she thanked them for all the help they had given her. They were happy for her that she was leaving, and they said they were going to miss her.

After she went back to her room, one of the nurses said to another, "I used to look at her in magazines, and envy her, she was so beautiful, and now I wonder what will happen to her."

"She'll be all right," the older nurse reassured her. "She's young, she'll come through it." But they both knew that wasn't always true. Victims of catastrophic events like the one she'd lived through often committed suicide, unable to adjust to the changes they had to face. At least Véronique had shown no sign of suicidal tendencies so far.

She had told them she'd be back for further surgeries. She intended to come back to the doctors she knew, and didn't want to try and find new ones in Paris. She didn't know anyone to recommend them to her, and didn't want to ask, and she had had enough medical attention to last a lifetime. She had no complaints about the treatment she'd had at the military hospital, but couldn't bear the thought of more operations.

She lay awake in bed that night, and only slept a few hours. She was torn about going home, both terrified and jubilant. In her heart of hearts she still magically believed that her mother would be there to greet her and tell her it was all a big mistake, she hadn't died and had been waiting for her in Paris all along. She knew that wasn't going to happen, but she kept hoping anyway.

She left quietly the next morning, with the nurses waving as she got into a taxi to take her to the train station. She had a small tote bag with her toiletries and her computer in it, some underwear they had given her at the hospital. She was wearing the clothes the nurse had bought for her, a pair of jeans and a gray sweater, a pair of navy blue sneakers, and she wore the surgical mask for the trip home. She felt as though she was returning to Paris as a stranger, not herself.

She bought her ticket for the TGV high-speed train to Paris, and watched the countryside rush past as she sat rigid in her seat, suddenly terrified that there would be an explosion on the train. She was shaking and she could easily imagine it happening. Images of the Zaventem attack kept flashing through her mind. There were beads of sweat on her face by the time the train slid into the station. She rushed from the train, and took great gulps of air to calm down the moment she got outside. Having survived the trip, it felt wonderful to be back in Paris. She hailed a cab, and on the drive to the seventeenth arrondissement, she saw all the familiar landmarks and nearly cried. She had thought she would never see her home again. So many times she had thought she would die in the hospital, and wished she had. She sat staring at her building when the cab stopped in front of it, and didn't get out for a minute.

"Is this the right address?" the driver asked her, and she nodded. He was puzzled by why she didn't get out. Most of his passengers were in a hurry, this one wasn't. She seemed to hesitate, as though she wasn't sure what to do next and was in a foreign land. She was savoring the moment and, at the same time, dreading having to enter the empty apartment.

Bernard had sent her a set of keys that Marie-Helene kept at the office for emergencies, since all of their keys had been lost at the airport. She held them now in a shaking hand, paid the driver, and finally got out. She entered the numbers for the outer door code, pushed the heavy iron doors open, and walked inside. She used an electronic badge for a second door, and slowly walked up the stairs to her mother's apartment on the second floor. The building was silent and empty at that time of day. There was a guardian who must have been having lunch. Véronique slowly unlocked the front door with shaking hands, and turned off the alarm in the unlit entrance hall and looked around. Everything was as her mother had left it. There was a navy blue wool jacket sitting on a chair, an umbrella in a stand. All the familiar antiques that Marie-Helene had inherited from her parents and Véronique had grown up with.

The woman who came to clean had kept the apartment dusted and in good order. There was a stack of mail, which Bernard's secretary came to pick up every week and went through, paying bills, opening correspondence, and throwing junk mail away. The door to her mother's little study was open and there was no sign of activity. She could see the living room with all the familiar furniture. The shades were drawn throughout the apartment. It all had a dry, brittle feeling to it, like a fallen leaf. The dining room was empty, and her own girlhood bedroom was down a hallway next to her mother's, with the kitchen at the end of the apartment. It was all there, but there was no sign of her mother, just as she had feared, and she had never felt so alone in her life. She sat down on a chair in the entrance hall, her legs were shaking hard, and she started to cry like the abandoned child she felt like. She pulled off the surgical mask, and her tears flooded her face and drenched her scars. She cried until she had no more tears to shed, and walked down the hall to her mother's bedroom. The bed was made and her slippers were underneath the night table. They were pink satin with a little ball of fluff on them. Véronique had bought them for her for Mother's Day the year before. It seemed like a lifetime ago.

She walked into her mother's small dressing room, and saw all her clothes hanging there, all the familiar things she had seen her mother wear, her business suits, her casual clothes for weekends, her favorite sweaters, the black velvet dress she wore on Christmas every year. It took Véronique's breath away. And when she walked into her own room, it was piled high with boxes, all the things that had been sent from her apartment. It was all here. She had come home again. But her mother was gone forever. She knew that now. Her fantasy hadn't happened. Her mother wasn't waiting for her. Her footsteps echoed in the empty apartment as she walked into the kitchen. She had no idea how she was going to survive living here without her mother. But she had to. She caught a glimpse of herself in a mirror in the hallway when she went back to her bedroom, and she saw the truth boldly staring at her, who she was now. She was no longer the girl people would stare at when she walked down the street because she was so beautiful, or whom they recognized because they had seen her in a hundred magazines. She was a stranger, even to herself. Half of her face was a reminder of those easy, happy days, and the other half was her reality of her present and her future. She was the girl who had survived a massive explosion, and had deep ugly scars to show for it. She would have to live with their shocked faces in future, and the jumbled memories of the worst day of her life, when she had lost her mother. Losing her beauty was the least part of it, and she would gladly have traded that if her mother had survived. But she hadn't. And in her wounded heart and soul, Véronique hadn't survived it either.

Chapter 6

Véronique spent her first night at home going through the boxes from her apartment. It had all been carefully and professionally packed by the movers. There were boxes of some books and papers, a few decorative items. She hadn't kept much at her apartment. The rest of it was mostly clothes, and she came across Cyril's things that he had left there when they went to Brussels. Some shirts, a blazer, jeans, a pair of beautiful chocolate brown suede shoes that looked very English. She put them aside, trying to decide if she should give them away or send them back to his mother. She thought it best to send them to her. She might want them out of sentiment, and Véronique didn't want to give them to strangers. She carefully put them in a box to send to her.

She went through the rest of her own clothes. She couldn't imagine wearing the evening gowns again. She no longer led that life and wouldn't be invited to black-tie evenings by Chanel and Dior. How could she wear an evening gown with a face like hers? It would be pathetic to pretend that her life hadn't radically changed. She put all the fanciest clothes away to save them. She wasn't ready to part with them, but didn't want to look like a freak or turn herself into a laughingstock or an object of pity.

She only put the most sober and unremarkable of her clothes on hangers, things she might actually wear, although for the moment she could only see herself in jeans and old sweaters with her surgical mask in place whenever she left the apartment. She couldn't eat in public with the mask, since it covered her mouth too, so she wouldn't be going anywhere, and she had no one to eat out with anyway. She didn't feel ready to call any of her old friends, nor the girls she knew while modeling. She was never close to any of them. Many of them had been jealous, and most models didn't work for long, and moved on, and so many of them were teenagers.

She spent the night organizing the closet in her childhood bedroom, and making piles to give away. She couldn't see herself in six-inch heels either, or satin evening shoes. They were no longer part of her lifestyle. She wouldn't be showing off anymore, or making appearances at gala events or invited anywhere. That was her reality now. She told herself it didn't matter. All that mattered was putting one foot in front of the other, and doing what she had to. She had reorganized her closets and the clothes she put in them by the end of the night, and fell into her bed gratefully. There was a big mirror over the dresser in her bedroom. She took it down before she went to bed, and replaced it with a painting she had always loved from her mother's bedroom. It was the portrait of a young woman, looking dreamily out a window, toward a green field that stretched into the distance. It had an airy, summery feeling to it, and reminded her of her mother. It had felt strange going into Marie-Helene's bed-room and taking it. Her mother's bedroom was larger than hers, but Véronique had no intention of moving into it. She was going to con-tinue sleeping in her own room.

When she woke in the morning, she had a heavy feeling, as though she had the weight of the world on her chest. Then she re-membered. She was home, and her mother wasn't and never would be again. Véronique felt as though she had returned as a different person. The person she had been six months before was a stranger, and was now as dead as her mother.

She spent the rest of the day opening the boxes from her old apartment. She picked up her mother's things left around the house, her glasses in the kitchen, a handbag she'd left in her study, a night-gown the cleaning woman had left folded on her bed, as though she would return. She put it all in her mother's dressing room, and de-cided to deal with it later. She wasn't ready to part with her moth-er's things yet. Her toothbrush and toothpaste were still in her bathroom, some old medications, her perfume and makeup, and some eye creams. Eventually, she'd have to throw it all away, but she couldn't bring herself to do it yet. She had another hard task to at-tend to first.

She called Bernard about arranging for the burial of her mother's ashes. She had decided not to have a memorial service. It would be too painful, even if it meant cheating her friends and clients of the opportunity to say goodbye. She'd already been gone for six months. Véronique wanted to bury her mother in private, with only Bernard present. She didn't want to have to explain the surgical mask to anyone. She felt selfish keeping it private for that reason, but she thought her mother would have understood, and given her the lee-way to do it as she wanted.

Véronique called the priest herself, and reached one she didn't know at their parish. Her mother hadn't been a regular churchgoer, but went from time to time when the spirit moved her. Véronique explained the circumstances to the priest, and he was shocked and deeply sympathetic. Bernard called to tell her that he had purchased a double plot at the cemetery, so that one day she could be buried with her mother, if she chose to. They had given him available times for a graveside funeral service, and she communicated them to the priest. They chose Friday in the late afternoon. The cemetery was a half hour out of the city, and Bernard said he could be there. He would bring the urn with her ashes with him, so Véronique didn't have to deal with it.

After calling the priest, she looked at the cellphone she had bought in Brussels, and turned it on so Bernard could reach her more easily, if he needed to, or the priest about the service. She went to make herself a cup of tea then, and chose her mother's fa-vorite brand in the cupboard. As soon as she sat down at the kitchen table, the phone came to life and started ringing. She answered it, assuming it was Bernard, and was stunned when the voice at the other end was her agent. She hadn't spoken to her since the day before she left for Brussels, when she had her last assignment. Ber-nard had notified them that she had been in the Brussels attack, but didn't tell her the extent of Véronique's injuries. He only said that she wouldn't be working for several months. He hadn't realized then that she would never work again. That had only become ap-parent when the last bandages came off her face, after the most recent surgeries. But he hadn't notified them, and neither had she. Véronique didn't want anything appearing in the press about it, and the hospital gave out no information. Véronique didn't want anything to make her sound tragic or pathetic. There had been no further press interest in her after the minor British tabloid ran the story about her, and somehow no other press service had picked it up. They had mercifully left her alone, and she had quietly faded from view over the summer. But it was September now and the fashion world would be busy. She knew that the waters would close over her soon enough. New faces would appear, new girls who would be the new top models. Her time had come and gone, and ended in Brussels. But her agent didn't know that yet.

"Is that really you?" Stephanie, her agent, said to her. "I was going to text you, but I decided to leave a voicemail. Your phone has been off for months," she said tartly.

"I was in the hospital for a while," she said, which Stephanie already knew, but didn't think it was serious.

"I know. Where are you now?" She sounded like she was talking to a schoolgirl playing hooky. Many of the models she dealt with were very young, even in their teens.

"I got back yesterday. I'm staying at my mother's." Véronique felt like a child as she said it.

"I left you alone for the summer," she said, sounding stressed and busy. "Thank God you're back, everybody wants you. We need you desperately. Fashion Week starts in ten days. Hell Week. I have nine designers who want you to walk in their shows, with fittings for all of them, of course. You can start next week," she said, sounding relieved. "We didn't tell anyone you were at the thing in Brussels.

Your attorney asked us not to when he called. Sensible. You didn't need an army of paparazzi at the hospital. We kept it very quiet. And now you'll be back. They don't need to know where you were. I assume you're fine now and ready to work." Not if they saw her face, Véronique thought. Stephanie didn't give her a minute to get a word in edgewise.

"I'm not walking this time," she said quietly. Or ever again.

"What? Why not? You have to. They all want you."

"I can't. And actually, Stephanie, I'm retiring." It took all of her courage to say it. It felt like jumping off a cliff.

"Did you lose your legs, or marry a billionaire? No other excuse is valid. We canceled the trip to Japan, and all your April and May bookings. And no one works in the summer. But you have to come back now. You can't retire. I won't allow it."

Véronique didn't want to tell her what had happened to her face. "I'm not up to it. I had my last surgery three weeks ago. And I still need more. I just can't do it. It's the right time for me to bow out." She tried to sound calm and sure about it.

"Bastards. You can't let them destroy a career like yours, just because you were in an attack. You're traumatized. But you're at the top of your game. Just do Fashion Week for me, and we'll come up with some excuse for a while after that. I can tell them you're pregnant. That will give you four or five months to finish your surgeries, and recover. Nothing too dreadful, I hope." She was home, so Stephanie assumed she was healthy enough to work for a week. And she sounded fine on the phone. Véronique didn't attempt to explain to her what had happened. Stephanie wasn't that kind of person. Ice ran in her veins, and hers was the best modeling agency in Paris.

She was all about the fashion business, and nothing else. She could make or break a career if she wanted to. She wasn't known for her compassion or kindness. She had girls working on the day of their parents' funerals, told them to dry their tears and put their big girl shoes on.

"I can't do it, Stephanie. I'm done. Not even for you. It's not possible."

"Careers can end very quickly, and you can't revive them. You'll regret this. Don't be foolish. The designers and the magazines will be pissed," she said in a taut voice, and Véronique wanted to get off the phone. Her threats were pointless. The terrorists had ended her career much faster than any designer could have, or even Stephanie. But she didn't want to be all over the tabloids with the truth, and become a tragic figure to be pitied. She had to live with the face she had now, and the consequences, for the rest of her life, and wanted to make her exit quietly, with dignity.

"The decision isn't reversible. I'm retiring, Stephanie. I want to leave on a high. It's not negotiable. I'm grateful for everything you did for me. It was fabulous, but I'm done."

"All you girls make such damn stupid decisions. You can't rewind the movie once you're out. Although with your face, you probably could. But you're taking a tremendous chance. Careers like yours don't happen often, and they can end overnight." The bombs had ended hers in seconds.

"I know that. They were the four best years of my life. I'm going to leave it at that. I'm still recovering from the trauma." She thought that might work better.

"The best way to do that is get back to work. I'm sure it was awful. But you'll just get depressed if you sit around and brood about it. I'll get you out of it this time. But you've already been gone for six months. Don't push your luck." She was fighting to keep one of the biggest models they'd ever had, and one of the best. She had never balked at work before, but Stephanie had no clue what Véronique was dealing with, or what she was asking. It would have been the shock of her life if she saw her.

"I do mean it. I'm done."

"Get some therapy, finish your surgeries, and stay in touch. I'll do what I can but I can't keep everyone at bay forever. There's always a new face that comes along and they fall in love with. You can become a piece of history in the blink of an eye. No one is irreplaceable."

"I know that. Thank you for calling. I'm sorry I can't do it for you. I would if I could." She tried to sound businesslike and firm, despite the knot in her stomach.

"Don't lose sight of what's important," Stephanie warned her. "Your career and your face on the cover of *Vogue* is who you are. Without that, you're nothing," she said harshly, but Véronique knew she believed it. She hung up then, and Véronique sat staring into space for a minute, thinking about what she'd said. That without her career, and her face on every magazine cover, she was nothing. If that was true, then she was nothing now, and she didn't want to believe that. Modeling careers didn't last forever, sometimes only for a year or two, or five or ten at best. So what happened to those women after that? They ceased to exist and became nothing? From her four years in the business, she knew that many models believed that they didn't even exist unless they were photographed and walked in the shows during Fashion Week.

Véronique's career had ended sooner than planned, but she didn't intend to stop existing because of it. She was still a person, a human being, and being beautiful was not the only thing she was capable of. There had to be more to life than that, whatever Stephanie thought. The value system was seriously flawed, and women believed it, that if they weren't beautiful, they didn't count. When their beauty faded, their life would be over. It was a myth that had women chasing the fountain of youth, spending fortunes to defy time and age, or desperate when they lost their looks. Véronique had lost hers brutally, violently, in less than an instant, but she could not allow her face to define her life, or her value as a human being. Being a model was every young girl's dream. It meant she was beautiful and validated her, and for the rest of time she would be chasing that validation to reassure herself that she mattered and was alive.

Suddenly, it didn't seem good enough. It wasn't enough to throw away all your values for. What about less attractive women? Didn't they have a right to be valid too, or did only the beautiful count in the game of life? Suddenly everything about it seemed wrong to Véronique. She wanted to prove Stephanie wrong. She hated everything those values represented, and didn't want to be a part of it. She had to find another way to validate herself, and live a life to be proud of. It was a turning point for her. Suddenly she needed air and wanted to get out of the apartment. She grabbed her mother's navy blue jacket, put it on, picked up her keys, and shoved her surgical mask in her pocket. She didn't want to wear it. She shouldn't have to. She didn't want to upset anyone with her damaged face, but she didn't want to be forced into hiding either.

There was no one coming in or out of the building when she left, and she turned down the street, and went for a walk, thinking about what Stephanie had said. All that mattered to her were the beauties. It was her business. But there were so many beautiful women in the world who didn't have pretty faces. Some of them shone from the inside, which seemed more important to Véronique now. Some people had a light that shone so brightly from within, you didn't even see their faces. Véronique wanted to be one of them, not be a model. She missed her face the way it had been, but maybe she could learn to live without it. Even without her lost beauty, she was a human being.

She was determined to try, as she drifted down the street, and passed a woman walking her small dog. She glanced at Véronique as she passed by and literally gave a start and backed away from her. She looked frightened, as though she was going to scream. It made Véronique want to run away, and hide, but she didn't. She went past other women with their dogs, and some didn't even notice her. Some were visibly shocked, and some men frowned when they saw her. A little girl stared at her, and said something to her mother that Véronique didn't hear. She must have asked her mother why Véronique's face looked like that.

She walked for a long way, and then turned around and headed home. She noticed all the reactions, the fear, the shock, the revulsion, and once or twice pity for whatever she'd been through. They could easily see, from the undamaged half, what her face had been before, but this was how it was now. It wasn't her choice. It had been done to her, a challenge she had to meet, and as she went back to her apartment, she knew that she couldn't let what had happened destroy her. The terrorists had gotten half her face, but she wouldn't let them have her soul too. As she stepped into the apartment, her cheeks flushed from the September air, and the scars on her face bright red, she knew that she was still whole. Who she was couldn't be taken from her.

Marie-Helene's funeral at the end of the week was as quiet and dignified as Véronique had wanted it to be. Bernard was there with her, and the young priest she didn't know. The cemetery workers had dug a small hole to put the urn in. The priest said a brief funeral service for her soul, a cemetery worker placed the urn in carefully, and they each threw a handful of earth in with it, and then Véronique took an Uber home, and Bernard went back to his office. It hadn't been as devastating as she had feared. There was a peaceful feeling to it, and a sense of loss, but she had a feeling of closure too.

She began sorting through her mother's clothes that night, kept some of her favorite things, and carefully boxed up the rest.

She had been working on it for a few hours when her cellphone rang. She still had her old number, but she hadn't had a call since Stephanie. She had faded from view for long enough that people no longer tried to call her, and had no reason to. She realized now that all of her calls before had been for work, or from her mother. Both had ended now. She couldn't imagine who was calling, and answered her cellphone, sounding distracted.

"Hi, beautiful. Who are you walking for next week? I just got in.

So how are you?" She recognized the voice immediately. He was a successful Irish photographer who lived in New York, Douglas Kelly. She had known him for all the years she'd been modeling, and had done several covers for *Vogue* with him. She always saw him during Fashion Week, whether they worked together or not. There had always been an undercurrent of romance with him, but it had never come to anything. She liked him better as a friend, and didn't want to spoil it.

"I'm okay, welcome back. I'm not walking for anyone. I retired. Stephanie wants to believe it's temporary, but it isn't. And how are you?"

"Holy shit, woman. What did I miss? What do you mean you retired?"

"I did. I just told Stephanie. She was pissed."

"Obviously she was. But that's ridiculous, you can't retire. You're the hottest face in the fashion business. I hope it's temporary. What brought that on?"

"It's a long story. It's a major life decision." She decided on the spur of the moment to tell him the truth, or part of it. "I had an accident."

"What kind of accident? You fell on your head, and have amnesia about who you are? Let me remind you, you're Véronique Vincent, the hottest model in fashion."

"Not anymore," she said quietly. "I'm done."

"Are you okay?" He sounded worried then. She sounded as though she meant it.

"I'm getting there. I just got home this week. I've been gone for six months. And I lost my mother. We just buried her today."

"Oh Christ, I'm sorry. That's rough. Should I call back tomorrow?"

"No, it's okay. She died six months ago. We waited to bury her till I got back."

"Where've you been for six months? Please don't tell me you're becoming a nun. I have a sister who's a nun, and one of the best models in New York entered a Carmelite order last year. It would be a terrible waste if you do that too. Besides, it would dash my hopes and evil intentions forever. Even I can't hit on a nun." She laughed. "So where the hell have you been?"

"In a hospital in Brussels."

"A mental hospital? At least that would explain the decision."

"No, I'm still sane. A military hospital."

"A military hospital? For God's sake, what's going on with you? Did you enlist?"

"I was at the Brussels airport, wrong day, wrong time last March."

"What were you doing there?" And then suddenly it hit him. He sounded shocked when he asked her. "Please God, don't tell me you were there during the terrorist attack." His voice was hushed when he asked her the question.

"Unfortunately, yes, I was. It's been a long haul. I just got out of the hospital. My mother was with me, and a friend. They both died when the first bomb exploded a few feet away from us."

"Oh my God, Véro, how bloody awful. I'm sorry about your mother. Are you okay? You didn't lose anything vital? I had no idea you were there."

"It was two weeks after Fashion Week. You'd already left, I guess. I'm okay. I'm full of shrapnel, but they say you can live with that, as long as nothing shifts. I had twenty-six surgeries. And all the moving parts still work and are still attached. A lot of people there weren't as lucky."

"Thank God, you're all right. Is that why you're not walking next week?"

"Yes," she said simply. "And I won't be anymore."

"I don't blame you, after something like that. It must shift your perspective about what's important in life. When can I see you? Are you free for dinner tomorrow night, or is that little British lord still following you around like a puppy?" She was quiet for a second before she answered.

"He died in Brussels. He was with me."

"Oh shit. I'm sorry. He was a sweet kid." Doug was thirty-nine, and Cyril had seemed like a child compared to him. "What about dinner tomorrow?"

"I can't do dinner." She couldn't eat with her surgical mask on, and she had no intention of showing him the right side of her face, or even telling him that part of the story. "Do you want to come to my place for a drink? I moved into my mother's apartment."

"Sure. Why not? I just want to see that you're okay after all that." She wasn't, but she was feeling a little better and it would be nice to see him. "Six o'clock?"

"That's fine." She gave him the address, and he was shaken when he hung up. What if she had died in Brussels too? He had read about the attack, and it was brutal. It made him realize as he often did how quickly life could change, in an instant. And clearly, she had thought that too. He wondered if she'd go back to modeling, or if she was finished for good. Everyone got burnt out eventually. It was an ephemeral, narcissistic business, and she had more substance than that. But she was also one of the great beauties, and he hated to see her give it up so soon. He couldn't wait to see her now. They had much to celebrate. She was alive. He was grateful that by some miracle she had been spared and survived the attack. You just never knew in life what would happen next. He had lived every day as though it were his last for years, and now she had learned that lesson too.

Chapter 7

Doug looked the way he always did when he showed up at Véronique's apartment. His unruly black hair seemed as though it hadn't seen a brush in a week, and he had a five-day growth of beard stubble on his face, which was the standard style for fashion photographers, and most men in the business. He was tall and thin, with lines around his eyes. He held her tightly in his arms when he hugged her, grateful that she was alive. She was wearing the surgical mask and he frowned when he saw it.

"What's that for?"

"Germs. I can't risk infection after all the surgeries." He nodded and believed her and assured her he wasn't sick if she wanted to take it off.

"I'm so relieved to see you. I couldn't sleep all night, thinking about you in Brussels. What a god-awful thing. I lost a friend at the Bataclan in November. He went to the concert and was shot and killed. These are crazy times." He glanced around after he said it. "I like your new apartment."

"I grew up here. It still feels strange being here without my mother." He nodded, sorry for her. From what he could see, she looked all right, but he noticed around the mask that she was very pale, and when she moved her arms, he could glimpse some nasty scars on her forearms and one wrist. He observed a big one on her ankle when she crossed her legs when they sat down. He poured a glass of wine for each of them.

"I ran into Stephanie today, by the way. I'm shooting for *Vogue* tomorrow, and she's sending me some new girl they want. Steph says you're traveling for a few months but you'll be back soon. I didn't tell her I talked to you. I was curious to hear what she would say."

"She suggested we tell people I'm pregnant to buy some time. I was very clear with her."

"Stephanie doesn't give up easily. She says she's had a million requests for you. She thinks being unavailable this time will only make people want you more. She's probably right. Are you sure you want to quit?"

"Yes," she said without hesitating, her eyes meeting his over the mask.

"That thing is very distracting," he said, pointing at the mask. "It's like talking to a woman in a burqa. I'm not sick or anything," he reassured her again.

"I'm not supposed to take it off. An infection would be dangerous for me." He couldn't argue with that. But his practiced photographer's eye noticed something unsettling at the edge of the mask near her ear, where the biggest scar started. He didn't dare ask her about it, until his second glass of wine.

"Are you hiding something under that mask, Véro? You can tell me, if you are." She hesitated for a second, as his eyes bore deep into hers. "You know I love you, even if you are smart enough not to go to bed with me. But I love you anyway." She laughed, and didn't answer his question. "What happened to you in Brussels?"

"I was a few feet from the bomb. A hell of a lot of shrapnel happened. They put me in a coma for three months, while they did most of the surgeries. They got a lot of the shrapnel out, but not all. And I've got some pretty nasty scars all over my body. I look like I got hit by a train. There's no way I could still walk down a runway in an evening dress. People would run for the exits screaming." She smiled as she said it, but he didn't.

"And nothing touched your face? That's amazing," he said, and watched her eyes intently as he did.

"I have a few there too."

"Is that why you're wearing the mask?" he asked her gently, and she didn't answer him at first. She thought about it, and then she nodded. He was her friend, and she trusted him. She had no one else left.

"You don't need to see that. It still looks pretty rough. I have two more surgeries coming up, but some of it is as good as it's going to get. I'm still getting used to it myself."

"You don't need to hide from me, Véro. We're friends. I was a medic in the army. I'm made of pretty strong stuff. The mask must be annoying," he said sympathetically.

"You get used to it. I went for a walk without it the other day, and several people looked as though they were about to scream. It's only on half my face. The other side is fine. The right side took a heavy hit."

"You don't need to wear a mask for me. You can take it off if you want. I promise I won't faint." He smiled at her.

"I nearly did when I saw it," she said, but she made no move to remove the mask. It was humbling to have him see how damaged she was now. She hadn't touched her glass of wine. She hadn't had a drink since the explosion and she wanted to be sober with him, although they had had some wild nights at parties they'd gone to. But those days were over for her now. It felt like her carefree youth.

He reached out and held her hand, and they sat there quietly, not talking, as she leaned against him. It felt good just being close to someone, and not having to pretend that she was better than she was. They sat there for a few minutes, and then she reached up and gently unhooked the mask looped around her ears. The left side of her face was toward him, the right side away from him.

"It looks fine to me," he whispered to her, still holding her hand.

"That side is fine," she whispered back. "It's the other side." And she turned slowly toward him, until he had the full view of what had happened to her. He didn't say a word for a minute, and then he nodded. There were tears in his eyes, but he didn't scream or react, or look horrified. It was heartbreaking to see what had happened, but he wasn't shocked, just sad for her.

"I'm not fainting. You're still beautiful, you know. Maybe a little more so, because you're not so perfect. Now can I take you out to dinner, since you don't have to wear that thing with me? Or we could both wear a mask and pretend we're doctors on a date?" She laughed, but it was as though someone had released all the tension in her body. He was right. She didn't need to hide from him. It was an incredible relief.

"You don't have to pretend it's okay. I know how ugly it is," she said sadly. She had looked at it a million times herself.

"What's ugly is that human beings do things like that to each other. That's the ugly part. The scars are just proof that you were there. There's no shame in that. You don't need to apologize for it, or protect people from it. Anyone who can't deal with it, that's their problem, not yours. What are they going to do? Blame you for it? Fuck them if they do," he said easily, and she laughed again. "And you can't wear a mask for the rest of your life, unless you want to become a surgical nurse. You're so damn gorgeous, with or without scars. Let them see your face. Just looking at you is a gift."

"You're crazy and blind, Douglas Kelly. How can you say that, with a face like this?"

"Because your face is still your face. You're still you. That hasn't changed. You're not just a nose and a cheek and a chin. You're you because of what's inside you. That's what people love. The rest is just very pretty window dressing, but it doesn't mean a damn thing. How many gorgeous girls have you and I both seen who're dumb as shit and mean as snakes, and real bitches? How beautiful is that, no matter how beautiful they are? I'd rather see your scars than look at them any day."

"I've been trying to think it through and make some sense of it. It's hard to do," she admitted, and he nodded.

"That's because doing that to another human being makes no sense. And we have this unreal image of what beauty should be.

Women are supposed to look like they haven't had a decent meal in ten years. They're so anorexic they make me feel sick. And their faces have to look a certain way. They have to be the right color, the right size, have the right size breasts, whatever is in fashion this week, tits or no tits. It's all bullshit and hype. The designers tell them what to wear, the experts tell them what they should look like. So they get a new nose, or a chin, or puff up their cheeks, or their asses or reduce their tits. Getting older is unacceptable so they get a facelift and seem like mummies or fill their face with Botox so they can't smile anymore. Or they blow up their lips till they look like Donald Duck. I'm so tired of shooting all that artifice and crap.

"Beautiful is beautiful no matter what happens to it. You are beautiful. You were then and you are now, and you'll be beautiful until you're a hundred years old, and you're beautiful even with a few scars on your face. So what? If I get a scar on my leg, will I be less of a man or a person, or less attractive? Hell, no. C'mon, let's go out to dinner and eat like normal people, or I'm going to get drunk on your wine, and I'll either pass out on your couch, or I'll make a pass at you and you'll throw me out. I'm starving." He stood up, and pulled her up with him.

"So am I," she admitted, smiling at him. "You really think I can go to a restaurant with this face?" she asked him innocently, and he wanted to put his arms around her and hold her.

"No, I think you should wear a bag over your head, and I'll show the waiter a photograph of how you looked before, and I'll eat your dinner too. Yes, I think you can go to a restaurant. Of course you can go to a restaurant. Ninety percent of the people there will be ugly, and never look as good as you do today. And you need to gain some weight, by the way. You don't have a professional excuse anymore. You look like they've been starving you at that hospital in Brussels. I'm taking you to feed you. Where do you want to go?"

They agreed on a nearby bistro. He called an Uber, and five minutes later they were out the door. Véronique wore a short fur jacket, and her jeans. She was just as beautiful as he'd said. She was a woman with scars. She wasn't just the scar itself.

Everything he had said to her that night was a gift. It had liberated her. She felt young and free as she got in the car with him. They had a good time at dinner. The waiter didn't bat an eye when he saw her. There were glances from a few people and then they lost interest and stopped staring, except for one man who continued to stare at her as they left the restaurant after an excellent meal. Doug stopped at his table, glared down at him, and tapped him on the shoulder. "They're dueling scars. Watch out for her. Don't piss her off. She's dangerous," he said, and then they left. The man seemed mortified. "I think I'm going to become your bodyguard to make sure people behave," he said to her when they were outside the restaurant. She was smiling broadly.

He dropped her off at home, and went on to the apartment where he was staying with a friend in the sixth arrondissement. "I'll call you tomorrow," he promised, and she knew he would. Doug had never disappointed her before, and he hadn't this time either. She walked into her building, and felt like a normal person, not a woman with a ruined face. He had reassured her, and she felt like herself again. She didn't look in the mirror when she brushed her teeth before she went to bed. She didn't want to spoil it. She slept well that night, and she woke up in the morning feeling good about life again. She didn't put her mask on when her mother's cleaning woman came. The woman didn't say a word or stare at Véronique's face. Doug had turned things around for her the night before and set her off down the right path. All she had to do now was hang on to what he had said and keep going.

She had a letter from her father in the mail that day. He thanked her for her letter, and said he would like to see her, if she came to New York. He said he hadn't been well recently, and was devastated to hear about her mother. It was a terrible end for a wonderful woman. He thanked Véronique several times for writing to him, and said he hoped to see her soon. His health was failing, and he said he would like to see her at least once before he died. They couldn't make up for lost time, but at least they could get to know each other, as much as time would allow. He said that her mother's untimely death was a reminder that one could never be sure of the future. He signed the letter "With love, Your Father."

It made Véronique cry when she read it. She wondered all day if she should go to New York especially to see him. He was right. The future was uncertain, and she didn't want to miss the chance.

She was still thinking about it when Doug called her, and invited her to dinner again that night. There was a place in Saint-Germain-des-Prés on the Left Bank that they had both always liked. She accepted with pleasure, and she told him about Bill Hayes over dinner.

"Bill Hayes, the senator, is your father? You never told me that," he said, surprised.

"I didn't know. My mother always told me he died when I was six months old. All I knew was that he was American, a lawyer, and she said his name was Bill Smith. She left me a letter for after she died, and it turns out that he was married. They fell madly in love, had me, and she left him so she didn't ruin his political career. He must have been pretty egotistical to let her do that, but he's my father and I'd like to meet him. I think she was in love with him for the rest of her life."

"He's supposed to be a pretty remarkable guy. I'd go meet him if I were you. He must be pretty old," Doug advised her.

"He's eighty-three."

"Go see him," he said immediately. They had another good meal and a fun evening. Fashion Week was approaching and they both knew he would be busy once it started. She wanted to be cautious. She didn't want to risk running into fashion editors or models or photographers she knew, or her agent. She was planning to lie low for the week, which Doug understood. People in fashion were such gossips. But she had been out twice with him now without the surgical mask and seemed perfectly at ease without it. He was pleased to see it. He meant what he had said to her.

After he dropped her off at her apartment, he went to meet the model he had shot for *Vogue* that day. She was twenty-one years old, and had hit on him when they were shooting. He knew himself well. He could never resist an open invitation like that from a pretty girl. In his line of work, he had all the women he wanted. He knew that Véronique knew what she was doing when she had always refused to sleep with him. She knew what a rogue he was, and he loved her for it. They were too far down the path of friendship now to turn back or change it, and the relationship they had suited them both and meant much more than his revolving door of one-night stands.

Véronique had suspected what he was up to when he mentioned the girl at dinner. She smiled as she let herself into her apartment. She was sure the twenty-one-year-old model would keep him happy for a night, and tomorrow there would be another one. That wasn't what she wanted with him. He was much better as a friend, and she intended to keep it that way.

In the morning, over breakfast, she decided to go to New York and meet her father. He and Doug were both right. The future was unreliable at best, and she wanted to meet him before anything happened to him.

She called and made a reservation for after Fashion Week would be over. She did not want to run into anyone she knew on the plane, and she wanted to see Doug while he was in town. She enjoyed his company and she never knew when he'd be back in town. His schedule was crazy and changed constantly when he got new assignments. She was always happy to spend time with him, and seeing her father could wait another week, although she was eager to visit him now that he had made contact, and wanted to meet her.

Véronique booked a flight to New York for two days after Fashion Week ended. That way she knew that almost all the New Yorkers would have gone home. The buyers and fashion editors who attended the shows rarely lingered in Paris. They usually rushed back to work in New York, so she assumed that the coast would be clear by then. Doug had finished his photo shoots too. He offered to go to the airport with her. He didn't say it, but he was worried that going to an airport might be traumatic for her. It would be the first flight she'd taken since the attack. She was grateful for his offer of help.

She hired a car and driver to take her, and Doug told her to stay in the car while he checked her bag in at the curb, and she watched from the car. Normally she'd have to do it herself, but he explained the circumstances to the baggage man, and pointed to her, and handed him her passport, and he nodded and took care of it.

"Does she need a wheelchair?" he asked sympathetically, and Doug shook his head.

"She can walk," he said softly, and Véronique questioned him when he got back in the car.

"What was that all about? What was he asking you?"

"He wanted to know if you had dope in your bag. I told him I smoked it all." He grinned at her and she laughed, and then looked serious as she glanced around at porters and passengers and ground crew rushing around the airport. It was all too familiar to her.

"I didn't think it would be so hard to be here. I keep thinking back to . . ." She didn't finish the sentence, but he knew. He could tell from the expression on her face. She looked terrified just sitting there.

"You should have flown with me," he said calmly, sitting next to her. But he was staying a few days longer to see friends, and he had a date with a stylist he'd met on a shoot. She was a beautiful Chinese woman who lived in London. Doug was a magnet for attractive women.

She stayed in the car for as long as she dared, and then he handed her her boarding pass with her luggage stub, and walked her inside as far as security. He wished she had gotten some kind of VIP treatment, but she hadn't asked for it, and didn't want to make a spectacle of herself. She had looped the surgical mask over her ears before she got out of the car, and he noticed several other people wearing them, particularly Asians, who were more germ conscious than most Europeans.

"You look a little neurotic," he teased her about the mask, and he saw that her eyes weren't smiling. She was deadly serious as she clutched her passport in her hand, and he could see that she was shaking.

"The alternative is worse," she reminded him. She hadn't worn the mask in Paris in several days, and was braver about going out without it now, thanks to him, but in close quarters on the flight, she didn't want people staring at her. She'd been both lucky and careful during Fashion Week, and stayed in her neighborhood and at home most of the time, so she didn't run into anyone she knew. A few people had mentioned her to Doug, and wondered where she had disappeared to. One British girl had seen the tabloid piece months ago, but most people didn't seem to know what had happened, and Doug just said he thought she was away for a few months. He knew Véronique didn't want him telling people she'd been a victim of the Brussels attack, if they didn't already know. Stephanie wasn't talking either, hoping she'd come back.

"Be good, and have a nice trip," he said when he hugged her, and kissed her on her good cheek. "Don't misbehave in New York. Say hi to your father for me." He grinned, and watched her thread her way into the security line. She gave a last wave, and he walked outside.

She had left the car for him, to go back to Paris. She really tore at his heart these days. She was being so brave, and so determined to recover, and he knew how hard it was. He didn't think he'd have weathered it as well. He wanted to do whatever he could to help her. He had given her the name of a plastic surgeon in New York one night at dinner. A model he knew had been mugged the year before, savagely beaten and stabbed. There had been a lot of damage to her face, and she looked remarkable now. He had called her to ask the name of her doctor. She said he was a miracle worker, and he'd given Véronique the name to consult him about her next surgeries. She was hesitant and said she trusted the surgeons in Brussels, but Doug had encouraged her and said it never hurt to get a second opinion. He hoped she had taken the number with her. She had never mentioned it again. She didn't like talking about medical issues with him. She was determined to learn to live with her altered face, rather than comb the world looking for surgeons who made empty promises and couldn't do anything about it anyway.

The chief military surgeon had already assured her that very little additional improvement was possible. The shrapnel had done too much damage, and the impact of the explosion too great. They were planning to fine-tune and smooth down some of the tissue around the scars, but they had warned her not to expect any major improvement on her face. Knowing that made her less inclined to consult another doctor. But she had brought the name of the doctor Doug had recommended just in case she wanted to see him anyway. There didn't seem to be much point.

* * *

The flight from Paris to New York was long and boring. She watched a movie and slept for a while. She didn't eat because she didn't want to take off the mask, and just took small sips of water, carefully lifting the mask toward her nose. She sat next to an American businessman who didn't attempt to engage her in conversation. He worked on his computer for the entire flight. When she was awake, she thought about her father, and what she had read about him. He seemed to be greatly respected as a family man and an honest politician. She wondered how different it would have been if the public had known about him and her mother. Her mother had freed him so he could maintain his immaculately clean image, which wasn't true. She wondered how many other politicians were like him, with well-kept secrets that would have destroyed their careers if they came to light.

She went through customs without a problem. The officer asked her to remove her mask if medically possible. She removed the loop on her right ear and looked him straight in the eye as he saw her scars, and he quickly told her that she could replace it and muttered, "I'm sorry." And then he glanced at her sympathetically. "Car accident?" he said softly. She was so beautiful that the contrast of the right side of her face had shocked him. He hadn't expected that, and assumed she was just another germophobe. A lot of people were, with flus rampant, especially during air travel.

"Brussels," she said in a clear voice. "Zaventem. The airport attack," was all she said, and he winced.

"I'm sorry," he said again, and she went through and picked up her bag, and found a cab at the curb.

She was staying at a hotel downtown she knew from when she

was modeling. Some big stars stayed there, Hollywood people, Europeans. It was trendy and fun, and all the best shops were nearby. She hadn't been shopping since she'd gotten back to Paris and didn't really want to. She didn't feel pretty anymore, and she wasn't going out. She'd been spoiled for four years, wearing fabulous clothes that designers loaned her for any occasion, or gave her after a shoot. She didn't need them anymore. She couldn't imagine going to a big fashion event again, and if she stayed out of sight for long enough, no one would invite her. She had been invited to two big parties during Fashion Week. She had declined. They had invited her because her name was on the guest list, but events like that were fickle, and she knew she wouldn't stay on their lists for long.

She checked in to the hotel, and took the mask off when she got to the room. She reached for the phone, out of habit, to tell her mother she had arrived safely. She always did that, so Marie-Helene wouldn't worry about her, or she texted her if she was too busy and went straight to a shoot or a party after she landed. She stopped with the phone in her hand, and realized that there was no one to call now. She was alone in the world, with only a father she hadn't met yet. But there was no one to care if she had arrived safely. It was a strange, empty feeling. She hung up the phone.

She ordered room service, and ate while she watched TV. She thought about meeting her father the next day. They had made an appointment by email. She wondered what he would think of her, if they would have anything in common to talk about. He had three children who he had given his time to for forty years. She was the unknown, the child no one knew about and never would. When she thought about it sometimes, she wanted to hate him, but she couldn't. If she hated him, there would be too many others to hate, and she couldn't afford that. She didn't want to hate the people who had destroyed her career and her face, and killed her mother. She walked a tightrope every day, to keep her balance, to stay on track, to look ahead and not back. Senator William Hayes was just another man she didn't know. She had survived without him for twenty-two years, and she would be fine without him again after she met him. She just wanted to see him once, to better understand the man her mother had loved, and why she had loved him.

Chapter 8

Véronique wore the surgical mask in the cab uptown to meet her father. Wearing it made her feel like an invisible person, as though people would look right through her because they couldn't see her face.

She wore a simple black Dior wool pantsuit, with a very chic jacket, and a simple white sweater. She wore high heels, which made her seem even taller, and she had her long chestnut hair loose in waves on her shoulders. She was able to wear eye makeup now, which made her eyes stand out above the mask. Her mother had always said that she looked like her father, and she knew it was somewhat true from the photographs, but he was an old man now, and maybe he looked very different.

He had an apartment on Fifth Avenue. It took them half an hour to get there in heavy traffic. A liveried doorman let her into the building, and announced her on a house phone, and an elevator man in uniform took her to the top floor. She had announced herself only as Miss Vincent. Her French accent was slight but detectable. Her mother had seen to it that her English was fluent. She had a distinctly French style about her. Four years as a top model had polished her appearance, and she looked very fashionable, as a butler answered the door, and led her into a small, handsomely decorated sitting room, with a view of Central Park. It was easy to note that her father lived well, and her mother had commented that he came from a wealthy family. She knew that he had gone to Harvard and little else about him, except what she had recently learned in her mother's letter and on the Internet. He had been a successful attorney and gone into politics, and the Internet informed her that he had had a distinguished career, so her mother's sacrifices hadn't been for nothing.

She was gazing out the window, thinking of her mother, when a nurse pushed an elderly man in a wheelchair into the room. He was wearing a dark gray suit, white shirt, and navy tie, with well-polished shoes, and impeccably groomed white hair. He stood up to greet her with warm eyes, and the smile she recognized instantly. He looked startled when he saw the mask. He held out a hand to her, and clung to hers, and then sat down in a large comfortable chair. He didn't look ill, but he seemed old and very frail. He was much taller than she was, and she tried to imagine her mother with him. He was so much older, and looked like an elder statesman. Her mother had been vital, almost twenty years younger, and looked young for her age. Véronique had never thought of her as old, even though she'd been forty-two when Véronique was born. Bill had been in his sixties, and looked his age now.

He waited until the nurse left the room, leaned toward Véronique, and spoke to her warmly.

"I've wanted to meet you for so long. I think your mother sent me every clipping from your modeling, and all your school photos before that. I have them all locked in a big box in a safe," he said with a wistful expression. He was studying her face then, and was puzzled by the mask. "I always thought that you look a great deal like my sister, Delia. She died in her twenties in a plane crash. We were very close." He was still holding her hand, which seemed like a surprisingly affectionate gesture for a first meeting, but there was no one else in the room to see it. "Are you ill?" he asked her gently, pointing to the surgical mask. "You don't need to worry about me. I'm not afraid of germs. I have a bad heart, but other people's germs don't make much difference."

"I was injured in the blast at the airport," she said simply, still holding hands with him. "It's upsetting to see, the scars are still very fresh. We were very close to the bomb when it went off, and I was filled with shrapnel afterward. They got quite a lot out, but not all, and it damaged my face," she said, and he looked pained hearing it.

"You don't need to hide it from me," he said gently. He seemed like a kind person. But if so, how could he have left them? That just didn't compute for her, and hadn't since she'd known. "I've been to a lot of natural disasters as a senator, and seen a lot of wounded people." She hesitated and then undid both loops, and put the mask in her lap. He saw both sides of her face at once. The perfect, untouched left side, and the fiercely damaged, scarred right. It allowed him to see what her face was like before, in person now, and what the bomb that had killed her mother had done. "Oh, my dear," he said sadly. He saw it as a tragedy, but Véronique gazed at him bravely, and then she bowed her head and spoke softly.

"I would give both sides of my face, and all my limbs, if my mother were still alive. She was so wonderful." He nodded, unable to speak for a moment with tears in his eyes.

"So would I," he said quietly. "She was much too young to die, and such a good person. She was the love of my life." He said it without embarrassment and Véronique was surprised that he was so open about it, after hiding it for so long. "I did you both a great in-justice. Politics are a powerful aphrodisiac, and a dangerous drug. I wanted to make a bid for the presidency, and your mother knew that. But the right opportunity and the right time never came. Look-ing back, it wouldn't have been worth it. I stayed in a loveless mar-riage, and I gave up the woman I loved, and our child. I stayed in touch with your mother, but we were very careful. We couldn't see each other. It would have been too dangerous. I gave up a reality for a hope, and your mother never blamed me for it."

"I think she loved you to the end," Véronique said softly. She liked him better than she wanted to, and she could see why her mother loved him. He appeared to be a kind, affectionate man, although maybe he had mellowed with illness and age, and he seemed more than willing to acknowledge his mistakes, and regretted them.

"So did I," he confirmed to their daughter. "It was always my dream to run for president. If I had to do it again, I would have given all that up. Men are foolish at times, and I certainly was. One of my children is running for Congress now. I tried to discourage him. You pay a high price for public life. What about you now?

What are you going to do without your mother? You're living in the apartment?" He had recognized the address on her letter. "You're not married? You're too young to be." He seemed fatherly for a minute. "Do you have a beau?" he asked her, and she smiled.

"No," and then she was serious again. "The man I was dating died in Brussels with us. And I'm not sure what I'm going to do now," she admitted, "with this," she pointed to the right side of her face. "Modeling is over for me. I'm trying to figure out what to do next. I studied literature and art history, but I'm not very interested in that. My mother made me go to the Sorbonne when I started modeling, so I could have a proper job one day. I don't know what to do. Maybe photography." She had been thinking about that, but hadn't done anything about it yet. "I'm still having some surgeries, and I have to go back to Brussels for that."

"You're all alone?" he asked, she nodded, and for a minute, she wanted to cry but held back her tears. "I know that Marie-Helene had no living family. Well, now you have me. You know where I am. If you need anything, I want you to call me. I'd come to Paris if I could, but it's too late now for that." She had read that his wife had passed away a few months before, and he'd had a heart attack around the same time. But he had his three legitimate children. "Are you seeing friends in New York?"

She shook her head. "I've only seen one friend since I got back from Brussels. I don't feel ready to deal with that yet. They're all in fashion, and they'll be horrified by my face. I came to New York to see you," she said simply. "I wanted to know what you're like, and why my mother loved you so much. I don't think she ever loved another man after you." But she had the same feeling about him now.

His whole face lit up when he talked about Marie-Helene. There were several photographs in the room of him with his wife. She was a distinguished-looking woman, even when she was young. Not a beauty, but a handsome woman. They stood next to each other in the photographs stiffly, like strangers, and neither of them smiled. It had struck Véronique when she glanced at them.

"Your mother and I were soulmates from the moment we met. If I hadn't been so foolish and ambitious then, we'd have married. But I was in my late fifties when we met, and I wanted to chase the dream before it was too late. It was a dream that evaporated in my hands. I enjoyed my time in the Senate, but it was poor consolation for what we gave up. And by then, it really was too late. It was too late to change my life in my seventies. My wife was ill by then, and our children would have been very upset."

Marie-Helene had managed well without him. Véronique knew it too. She had never depended on anyone but herself, and had provided a strong, loving foundation for their daughter. Marie-Helene was never needy. She was a proud, intelligent woman who would never have begged him to come back. She had never asked him for anything, and what he had given, he had given from his heart, for their daughter. There had been no room in his life for them then, but he had broken two hearts in the process, his own and Marie-Helene's.

He asked about her schooling and her friends, and she said that her mother had always been her best friend. He got a sense of the immensity of the loss for her, which was even greater than his own. He asked about the money she had made as a supermodel, and she said that her mother had invested it well for her.

"She had a great head for business," he complimented her. "We couldn't see each other, because of the press, but we spoke fairly often. I always asked her advice." In an odd way they had been life partners for twenty-four years, even though they weren't together. "My wife and I were very different. She was more interested in her horses than anything. She was a great horsewoman. She hated politics, and she wasn't even very close to our children. She didn't have it in her. She was more interested in bloodlines and horseflesh than people." She got the sense that he had been a lonely man, and increasingly she was understanding the bond between her parents that even time and distance hadn't been able to sever. She realized that she really had been their love child, in the best sense of the word.

As the afternoon wore on, she could see how tired he was getting, and she didn't want to wear him out. He started coughing a lot, and she told him she should go. He looked sad when she said it, but he didn't ask her to stay longer.

"Will you come to see me again?" he asked her, holding both her hands and looking into her eyes, which were identical to his own.

"I will," she said softly. "Thank you for seeing me today." She didn't know what to call him, "Senator" seemed silly, and "Dad" presumptuous, and foreign to her. He seemed to read her mind.

"You can call me Papa, if you like. That's how your mother referred to me when I played with you when you were a baby." She smiled and nodded, it sounded just right to her. It was what her friends had always called their fathers. It occurred to her then that now she knew what she had missed. It was bittersweet, as she helped him stand up, and get back in his wheelchair. "You're a wonderful girl, Véronique. I owe a great debt to your mother. It's a gift just seeing you today. And you know, those scars don't make any difference. You're still a stunningly beautiful girl, and they will probably fade some in time."

"That's what the doctors say, but they're pretty awful."

"You don't need to wear that mask, or be ashamed," he said, as she got ready to put it back on. "I think you're brave enough to face the world without it. You're a great deal like your mother. She was the bravest woman I ever knew." He kissed Véronique's hand then, and she bent down to kiss his cheek where he sat in the wheelchair. "When are you going back to Paris?"

"Tomorrow night." The visit had been perfect. Better than she had hoped it would be.

"Come and see me again when you're back in New York." He smiled at her, and pressed a bell, and the nurse reappeared. He was beaming when Véronique left him. She walked into the hall, as the nurse wheeled him away. She had a lot to think about, as she got in the elevator and left the building a few minutes later. She had been with him for almost three hours. She walked down Fifth Avenue for a while, thinking about her father. She had no question in her mind now about why her mother had loved him. She was only sorry that they hadn't made a life together, and he hadn't been courageous enough to give up his dreams and his wife. But her mother was a wise woman, and he might have resented her if he had. She had set him free, and kept his heart. Theirs had obviously been a great love story, and Véronique was profoundly happy to have met him. She hoped she would see him again, and wished they lived in the same city. His health seemed so precarious that she wasn't sure they would meet again, but she had taken enough from their visit, that she knew it would keep her warm for a long time. She guessed that her mother had felt that way too, and she'd had Véronique as part of him. That must have helped. She understood their relationship better now. Even at his age, he had immense charm.

She walked for a long time, and then took a cab the rest of the way downtown to her hotel. She hadn't bothered to put the mask on, and she saw the driver glance at her in the rearview mirror, but he didn't comment. When she got back to her hotel, and searched for her room key in her bag, she found the paper where Doug had written the name of the plastic surgeon in New York. She looked at it for a minute when she was back in her room, and hesitated. She didn't know if she wanted to call him or not. The Belgian surgeons had been so definite that little improvement was possible, if any, that it seemed pointless. And then, in an optimistic mood after seeing her father, she decided to put it in the hands of fate. She called, and told herself that if there was an appointment the next day, before her flight, she would take it, and if not, she'd forget about getting another opinion. She didn't want to spend the rest of her life, or even the next few years, chasing doctors with empty promises, who offered her results they couldn't deliver. It would be a life of constant disappointment. She was trying to accept the hand she'd been dealt and make the best of it. That seemed more sensible.

The phone rang and a receptionist answered. "Doctors Talbot and Dennis," she said, and Véronique said that she was hoping for an appointment for a consultation with Dr. Talbot, who had done the work on Doug's model friend who'd been mugged. She was sure they wouldn't have room for her on a day's notice, and was prepared for a rejection.

"Please hold," the nurse said, after Véronique told her it had to be the next day, since she was flying to Paris that night on a late flight. She came back on the line a full five minutes later, while Véronique waited. "We don't have a regular appointment available till February, but we had a new patient cancellation at ten-fifteen tomorrow. Can you make it?" His office was on Park Avenue at Sixty-ninth Street, so she would have to go back uptown, but she had nothing else to do. She wasn't shopping and had no one to see all day before her flight.

"Yes, I can," Véronique said, almost sorry she'd called him. She didn't want to deal with more doctors. It had been a stupid idea, she decided, but she'd stuck her neck out now.

"Please come to the office at ten so we can get a new patient history and insurance information." She didn't bother telling the receptionist that she'd pay cash, or by credit card, since she didn't have American insurance, and had no reason to. All her expenses so far had been paid by the Belgian government, or she could have been treated in France for free if she preferred, with her carte Vitale, which paid for all medical fees.

The receptionist hung up then, and Véronique sat quietly, thinking about her father again. She would have liked to see him again before she left, but with his poor health, it seemed like too much to ask of him. He had looked drained when she left him, but happy to have seen her. She decided to call him to say goodbye, but not ask for another meeting so soon. They had said everything they needed to today. He had told her everything she had always wanted to know about him, and her mother.

The best part about seeing him was that for the first time in her life, she felt like she had a father. Papa. She liked the sound of it. She had never missed him before, she had only been curious about him. But now she knew who he was, and although he barely knew her, she could sense that he loved her. Knowing him now was a tiny consolation for the enormous loss of her mother, but it was something. He felt like a living link to her mother. He had been her mother's final gift.

Chapter 9

It took Véronique an hour to get uptown to see the doctor. New York was one giant snarl of cars at that hour. She took a magazine with her to read in the cab, and she was nervous about the appointment. She had seen enough doctors to last a lifetime. She had no idea why she had allowed herself to add one more. But Doug had been so insistent about it. She was in New York anyway, and they'd had the cancellation. But it seemed like a waste of time, as she got out of the cab and walked into his street-level office. She was startled when she walked inside. There was very expensive contemporary art on the walls. A Damien Hirst, a Julian Schnabel, and two large Diebenkorns. The office was mostly white and soothing pale colors, except for the art. There were comfortable oversized chairs by a well-known Italian designer. Everything about the office shrieked money. The nurses were wearing crisp little white suits, and Chanel flats. The women in the waiting room wore expensive exercise clothes, and chic outfits. There were women there of all ages, and she guessed that most of them were there for fillers and Botox shots. She knew that many of the models she had worked with started Botox in their twenties to smooth out their faces and prevent lines. They were all obsessed with fighting the aging process even before it began. Véronique had never bothered with any of it. It seemed stupid at twenty-two, or whenever they started. There were a few middle-aged women in the waiting room, but not many, and Véronique was suddenly worried that models she knew might walk in and recognize her. She hadn't bothered to wear the surgical mask for the appointment.

She filled out the paperwork quickly, and was ushered into a large office, with more impressive art, a sleek ebony desk, and a forest of exotic white orchids along one wall. In less than five minutes, Dr. Phillip Talbot walked in. He was tall, blond, and handsome, with a slight tan, piercing blue eyes, perfect teeth when he smiled, and he looked like a movie star or a model. Véronique had worked with hundreds of men who looked like him, and he was every bit as handsome as they were. She saw that he was wearing a wedding band, which she suspected must have disappointed many of his patients, and she guessed him to be in his early or mid-forties. He was wearing a white doctor's coat over gray slacks and Gucci loafers, with a perfectly tailored white Hermès shirt and no tie.

"Sorry to keep you waiting," he apologized, smiling at her as he breezed into the room and walked to his desk. She hadn't been waiting more than three minutes. "We try to keep things rolling on time here. Everyone's busy." He had a wide dazzling smile, in keeping with the rest of his good looks. And he seemed just professional enough, and just friendly enough, to satisfy his very high-end clientele. He had numerous clients in fashion, and many movie stars and socialites, and was known for his discretion. He glanced at her chart and saw her name. "Véronique Vincent? The model, I assume." He had no visible reaction to the right side of her face, and spoke to her as though her appearance was entirely normal. She nodded.

"Yes, but not lately. I retired." He could see why, but didn't comment. He was extremely professional and personable, just the right degree of both.

"How can I help you today?" He was wise enough not to assume that she was there about the damage to her face, if she had come for some other reason. That happened sometimes, and he waited for her to tell him.

She got right to the point, not to waste his time, or her own, and she wasn't hopeful. "I was in the attack at the Brussels airport in March." He nodded, with a serious expression, knowing that the damage undoubtedly extended far beyond her face, and had included many complicated injuries and internal damage, as well as the psychological trauma. "I was hit by a great deal of shrapnel, very close to where the bomb exploded." She went down the list of her injuries and the organs that had been affected. "I was kept in a coma for three months, and had twenty-six surgeries. I'm due for another one in December or January, to try to soften the scars on my face, but they've already told me there's not much more they can do. A friend suggested that I come and see you. I was in a military hospital for six months, and just got out in September. I thought I'd see you before my next surgery, and see if you agree with the procedure they have in mind. They want to do another surgery after that too, but they said that the improvement will be very slight." He looked very serious as she shared the information with him. The casual air and broad smile were gone.

"You've been through an awful lot, Véronique," he said. "May I call you by your first name?" She nodded assent. "I've read about it, but I haven't seen any of the victims here in the States. I think most of them were treated locally. But from what I've read, and what I know about similar events, you were in exactly the right hands. Injuries like the ones you sustained, from a bomb detonated at close range, with additional enhancement, are best treated in military facilities, because they most resemble wartime injuries and not civilian ones. So I will assume that you got the very best treatment possible in Brussels.

"As far as the damage to internal organs and loss of limbs, a military facility has all the right expertise to deal with that. Where they might fall short is when you get down to cosmetic issues, which may be less sophisticated in the military than what we do here for patients with more delicate issues, and high-profile lives. A combination of both disciplines could be very effective for you," he said encouragingly, "and may get you better results now than what they can offer you at this stage of your recovery. I assume you must have some scars on your body and limbs as well." She nodded and pulled up the sleeves of her sweater. The scars were still angry and peppered both her arms. Some were quite large, but she had learned to live with them so far, and kept her arms and legs covered all the time. She told him about the surgery they were intending on her face in two months, and he nodded. "Let's have a look, shall we?" He turned a light toward her, which shone brightly.

"My right eye is affected too. I see shapes and light now. They saved the eye, but I have limited vision from it." He looked unimpressed by her injuries, as though he saw worse every day, which made her comfortable. He didn't seem shocked, or overly sympathetic, which so many people did. He just treated her like any other patient, not a miracle to have survived a bombing.

"I can see why they recommended the procedure they did, but on fine features like yours, and very fine skin, I think we can get you better results with a more delicate procedure. It's no more involved for you as a patient, it's just a little more work for us in the surgery. I agree that we can't eliminate the scars completely, but I think we could get you a pretty satisfactory result, with a different process. We won't need to keep you in the hospital for more than a few days. And I'd want you here for a few weeks so we can watch your recovery for complications. And then a second surgery about three months later, and we can reassess things after that." She liked him immediately, and what he said made sense, also the fact that models and actresses and movie stars needed different results than ordinary soldiers would have. She felt as though she had come to the right place, thanks to Doug. "You're still living in Paris?" he asked her.

"Yes, I am."

"You could fly in and fly out, and we have apartments we lend our patients who come from far away. It's included in the price of the surgery, with maid service, and a restaurant nearby that caters. You might be more comfortable there than at a hotel. It's more discreet. You can think about it, and let me know what you decide." He flipped through a leather appointment book on his desk, to check his surgical schedule, and then looked up at her. "I have an open day you probably won't like. The twenty-second of December. It will mess up Christmas for you, but I have fewer surgical patients then, for obvious reasons, and I'll be on call through the holidays, so I can keep an eye on you post-op myself, and you should be able to go home in mid-January, maybe sooner. With the follow-up surgery in March, whenever it's convenient for you." He made it all so easy for her, and she realized Christmas would have no meaning for her this year. "You'll be bandaged of course, but you can go out in a few days. Will that screw up your Christmas plans too badly?"

"I won't have any. I don't have any family. My mother died in the attack, so maybe it would be a good time to do it," she said, and he nodded, and smiled at her again.

"I don't want to press you into it. Why don't you give it some thought and let me know? I think we can get you a pretty good re- sult. It won't be perfect, or look the way it did before, but I think we can get a very satisfactory outcome to smooth things over, and calm things down." As he said it, another man in a doctor's coat walked in, he was shorter and had dark hair and chocolate brown eyes and looked like a teddy bear. They were an interesting contrast to each other. The other doctor looked about fifty. Phillip Talbot introduced his partner to her.

"This is my associate, Dick Dennis. He does great bodywork, if you ever want to clean up the scars on your arms and legs," he said casually with a warm smile, and Dr. Dennis rolled his eyes.

"He makes me sound like a mechanic at a used car dealership." He smiled at Véronique too, and Dr. Talbot explained to him in very dry technical terms about the bombing and her injuries. He also recognized her name immediately and knew who she was. She was even more beautiful than in her photographs, he thought but didn't say. He was shocked by the scars on her face but didn't show it.

"She's considering some retouching on her face in December, she's going to think about it." She liked them both so much that she wanted to stay and let them do it now, but it was too soon. Her last surgery was still too recent, and it made perfect sense to her that the kind of facial surgery Dr. Talbot did would be more refined than what they did in the military. "She might be spending Christmas with us." He smiled at Véronique and his partner.

"We'll let Santa know where you are," Dick Dennis promised. "I'm sorry to barge in, Phillip. I wanted you to look at some photographs for me. I'll leave the file with you." He put it on Talbot's desk, and Véronique liked the way Phillip Talbot had referred to her surgery as "retouching," like a photograph that needed correcting. The way he phrased it made it sound less frightening, and not as grave. Everything they had done in the military always sounded so terrifying, and they were so pessimistic about the results, particularly about the scars on her face.

"Could we do some bodywork at the same time?" she asked cautiously. "I wasn't really planning to do that, but some of the scars are pretty bad, especially on my back and stomach. There were huge chunks of metal flying everywhere. And my arms look awful. I just keep them covered."

"Would you like me to have a look?" Dr. Dennis asked her, and she nodded.

"Do you have any other questions for me?" Phillip Talbot asked her.

"I don't think so. You explained everything." She smiled shyly at him, and he took out his card, jotted his personal cellphone number on it, and handed it to her.

"Just let me know if you plan to spend Christmas with us. If not, I'll try to find another date that works for you, but it may not be till the end of January."

"I'd rather not wait," she said. She was excited about trying what he suggested. She knew her face wouldn't be perfect, and never would be again, but better would be wonderful, and she was very impressed by both of the surgeons. She and Dr. Talbot shook hands and she followed Dr. Dennis out of the room to an examining room, where she carefully removed what she was wearing, and stood in her bra and underpants, and turned slowly so he could check all her scars minutely. He used a magnifying glass on some of them. He looked at her seriously afterward.

"The force of the blast must have been tremendous. I think you got lucky with the one on your left foot. You could have lost a foot, or even your leg."

"They operated on those right away. Apparently, I almost did lose the foot, but they saved it. And the one on my stomach is where I lost part of my liver. I had metal lodged all through my body, and still have quite a lot, but they got a lot of the shrapnel out in the twenty-six surgeries." Even as a doctor, he couldn't imagine what going through it must have been like.

"You're a very brave woman," he said. "I have a daughter your age. I would be beside myself if something like that happened to her. I assume you had therapy at the hospital while you recovered."

"I did, but I wasn't brave. I was in a coma for three months. They did most of the surgeries then, so I was asleep. It was harder when they woke me up." She had marks all up and down her arms and legs from the constant IVs.

"How much of it would you want to work on?" he asked her gently.

"Maybe just the worst ones for now, when I get the surgery on my face. They did cosmetic work on my face in Brussels, but not on the scars on my body."

"I can see that. We'll do a little sanding and polishing," he said, smiling at her, "and see how you feel about it afterward. Dr. Talbot will do a wonderful job on your face. It's what he does best. As he told you so inelegantly, I do the bodywork." He did mostly tummy tucks and breasts, but she didn't need either. And liposuction on thighs and buttocks, none of which was relevant for her. She had a flawless body, along with her perfect face, except for the scars she had everywhere now from the shrapnel. It was a crime to see what had happened to her, but in spite of the damage, she was a stunningly beautiful young woman, and he wanted to help restore her to something closer to what she had been. "I look forward to seeing you if you come back to us, Véronique," he said kindly. "I'd be in the surgery with Dr. Talbot. The recovery will be fairly quick, much faster than what you went through while you were in critical condition." It all sounded appealing to her, and she liked them both. She had liked her surgeons in Brussels too, but they were more serious and more military, and not as polished and friendly. She had fallen into a very high-end practice, one of the best in New York. She was excited about what they might be able to do, and they gave her a glimmer of hope for the future.

She was smiling when she thanked Dr. Dennis, and left the office a few minutes later. It was the most hopeful thing that had happened to her since the bombing.

She went over to Madison Avenue, and walked almost all the way downtown to her hotel, looking in the shop windows. She stopped at one of them, and bought a bright red sweater, which suited her mood. She had been wearing subdued colors, she realized, so as not to draw attention to herself, and suddenly she felt fine about it. She felt like she was coming back to life. She could hardly wait until Christmas. She wanted to call and tell them that she wanted to have the surgery, but promised herself to think about it, and not make a hasty decision. She'd loved everything she'd heard at the appointment.

She was in great spirits when she got back to her hotel, and decided to call her father and tell him about it. The butler told her that Senator Hayes was resting and couldn't be disturbed. He'd had a difficult morning. She hoped she hadn't contributed to it by wearing him out the day before, and left a message saying that she hoped he felt better, and sent him her love. He had told her that she could call him anytime, and she had taken him at his word, and hoped that was all right.

She spent the rest of the day taking it easy and thinking about everything the two plastic surgeons had said. They had given her a glimmer of hope for the first time in months. A hope that she might look even slightly more normal again. She walked around SoHo in the late afternoon, went back to the hotel for an early dinner, and left for the airport in time for her evening flight to Paris.

She was standing in the airport, waiting to board her flight, thinking about the past twenty-four hours, seeing her father, and the doctor's appointment that morning, and she knew that she didn't want to wait any longer to book the surgery. She took Phillip Talbot's card out of her purse, and called him on his cellphone. It was nine o'clock at night, but she didn't want someone else to get her slot for the surgery.

He answered immediately and she said who it was.

"I'm sorry to call you so late, but I wanted to tell you, before I fly back to Paris. I would like to do the surgery on December twenty-second, as you suggested. And Dr. Dennis said that he could do some of the scars on my body too."

"Well, that is good news, Véronique. We'll be very happy to have you with us for Christmas. Would you like me to book one of the guest apartments for you?" He made it sound like a fun weekend and a party, not surgery.

"Yes, I would," she said, feeling breathless. She would never have thought that she would be excited about surgery. He had already told her that the surgery itself would be performed at NewYork-Presbyterian Hospital, and she would spend three nights there before moving to one of their guest apartments to continue the recovery. The apartments sounded extremely plush and comfortable, and she was sure they were. She also wanted to ask him the cost of the surgery, since she had no insurance that would pay for it. She was going to use some of the money her mother had left her. She was sure her mother would have been happy to know how she was using it.

"I'd like to know what the fees will be for the surgery, so I have some idea. I can send a bank wire before I come over."

He sounded serious when he answered. "Dr. Dennis and I dis-cussed it after you left, Véronique. None of this should ever have happened to you. There is a terrible injustice about it. We're going to do the surgery for free. We both want to do that. It's our Christ-mas gift to you. You'll have to pay for the hospital stay, but our fees and the use of a guest apartment are a gift. We can discuss fees for the next time, but this one's on us." She was stunned and had tears in her eyes.

"I don't know how to thank you. You were both so kind to me today. I'm really excited about the surgery."

"It won't be perfect," he reminded her, so her expectations wouldn't be unrealistic, "but we think you'll be happy with the re-sult. You'll need to come in the day before for some lab work. So we'll see you on December twenty-first."

"Thank you, with all my heart," she said, and ran for her plane after she hung up. There were still truly good human beings in the world, and clearly the two doctors she had met thanks to Doug were among them. She felt as though she were flying herself when the plane took off. After that, she slept all the way to Paris. It had been a fantastic visit to New York.

Chapter 10

After feeling euphoric when she left New York, her arrival in Paris was harder than she'd anticipated. She let herself into the apartment at noon and unconsciously expected to see her mother come out of her bedroom, or hear her in the kitchen, making coffee and something to eat. It was a Saturday and she should have been home. Instead, the apartment was dark and empty, the shades were drawn, and there was silence. It was crushing it was so quiet, and the reality that her mother was gone hit her all over again. Her heart felt like a lead weight in her chest as she put her suitcase down in her own room, and walked around the apartment, looking for some sign of life. There was none. There was silence and darkness everywhere, and the weather outside was gray.

She sat down in the kitchen, trying not to cry, and her cellphone rang. She hesitated, and then answered it. The caller had used a blocked number, so she had no idea who it was, but it was a relief

to hear a human voice. She was startled to hear that it was a Swed-
ish model she knew and hadn't seen in two years.

"It's Ulla," she said exuberantly, and Véronique was sorry she'd
answered. They had never been friends. "How are you? I'm finally
working again. I had twins, but I'm back now. I just thought I'd say
hello. Are you very busy?" She was a nice enough girl, but Véronique had never been close to her and had no idea why she had
called her.

"Actually, I'm not modeling anymore. I took some time off."

"Pregnant?" she asked, laughing.

"No, I just needed some time off. I just got back from New York."

"I'd love to see you. My mother is keeping the twins for two
weeks, so I could take some jobs here. I missed Fashion Week. How
was it?"

"I don't know. I wasn't here." She had been, but she'd been hiding.

"I had to have my breasts done after the twins. Nursing is a disaster. I won't make that mistake again. And it took me a year to lose
the weight. But it was nice being at home in Sweden with my
mother." Véronique assumed that Ulla wasn't married to the twins'
father. "I couldn't have done it without her. I'm going to have some
work done on my face when I'm here. I need fillers, and I'm doing
Botox shots now. I've been doing some fantastic electro massages on
my face in Sweden. It's almost like a facelift." Ulla was twenty-nine
years old, and was approaching the end of her career. Already, before she'd left, she'd been getting fewer calls, and the demand for
her had dwindled. She had been spectacular looking at seventeen,
but twelve years later less so.

They talked for a few minutes, and Véronique got off the phone as gracefully as she could. The conversation reminded her of what Doug had said about how tired he was of girls obsessed with their weight and their age, getting Botox shots at twenty-two, and fillers, and surgery, enlarging or reducing their breasts, starving to keep their weight down, and terrified they would get a line or a wrinkle. It seemed an insane way to live, and totally narcissistic. It was all that most of them talked about. Véronique was twenty-two and had been at the height of her career, but in five years that might not be true. She missed the fabulous jobs for Dior and Chanel, walking in their shows, being on the cover of *Vogue*, photographed by every famous photographer in the world. But how long did it last and what did it mean? And what happened to all of them when it was over?

Only a handful of the very famous ones lasted into their thirties. The others were considered old at twenty-five, and were competing on the runway with fourteen- and fifteen-year-olds who were hired because of their coltish looks and had no curves yet. It was an express train you couldn't chase and still climb aboard. And when it was over, the editors and the agents and photographers were heartless.

Véronique wondered if maybe she had been spared the embarrassment of a career that would end suddenly one day when a line appeared somewhere and her body was no longer flawless. Hers was intensely flawed now, and battered and wounded beyond belief. She had been blown to bits by the bomb that had ended her career instantly. But the slow death of rejection because she was considered too old at twenty-six wouldn't have been pleasant either.

It was a crazy business, and the standards they set weren't human. Real humans and normal women didn't look that way, they didn't starve the way models had to, or take drugs to lose weight, have their feet superglued into shoes so they fit even if the size was wrong, and then have their feet bleed when the shoes were torn off. Véronique had lived through all of it in the early years at eighteen and nineteen, and then the rocket-ship ride to stardom at twenty, until she was the most successful model in the business. But at what price glory?

She hated the way her career had ended, and she would have gone back if she could have. But she wondered now when she would have tired of it, and how it would have felt when they stopped begging her agent for her for magazine covers and shoots in exotic places. It all seemed so ephemeral, and made her ponder again what she was going to do now. She needed some kind of job eventually, but with a face as severely damaged as hers, who would hire her, even for an office job? She had no experience with children and her face would terrify them. And unless Phillip Talbot could create a miracle in New York, she'd have to find a job hidden away somewhere, where no one would see her. She no longer met anyone's standards for beauty.

She was feeling sorry for herself, crushed by her mother's absence in the apartment that afternoon, when Doug called her. He wasn't sure if she was back yet, but decided to try. He was still in Paris for a few more days.

"How was New York?" he asked when she answered the phone. "Did you see your father?"

She sounded peaceful. "He was amazing. He really is a nice man, and it's too late now, but he says he regrets the choices he made. He never got where he wanted in politics. I guess he had his eye on the presidency when my mother was with him. He gave up everything for that, including the love of his life, and stayed in an empty marriage. He's very old now, and he's pretty sick. He was really nice to me, though, and we spent about three hours together."

"I'm glad for you, Véro. At least you met him, and heard his side of the story."

"My mother didn't like to talk to me about him, but she always said nice things about him when she did. She didn't hate him for leaving us. Maybe she figured that if he gave up his dreams to be with us, he'd wind up hating her for what he missed."

"It's amazing the shit choices we all make sometimes, and then end up paying for the mistakes forever. It's why I think I'll never get married. It's too big a commitment. How the hell does anyone know at thirty what they'll want or who they'll be at fifty or sixty?"

"But if you don't make the commitment, you wind up alone, and that's not so great either." She was getting a taste of it now and she was lonely.

"I think I like alone better," he said. It was why she had never wanted to be involved with him romantically. Doug was never going to settle down or make a serious commitment. He claimed that he felt the same way about it at thirty-nine as he had at twenty. Nothing had changed.

"I met someone else, by the way." She sounded brimming with excitement when she said it. "I called the doctor whose name you gave me, from your friend, Phillip Talbot, the plastic surgeon."

"Now that *is* interesting. What did he say?"

"He said he thinks he can do some things to improve my scars. He can't erase them completely, but he says he can soften them and make them look less extreme. It won't be perfect, but it will be better. It sounds like a better version of what they were going to do in Brussels next time. I think his techniques are a lot more refined and sophisticated."

"So is his clientele," Doug said sensibly, and she agreed. "My friend's face looks fabulous now, and it was a disaster before. She still has some slight scarring, but nothing like it was. She can cover hers with makeup," which Véronique knew she couldn't. Her scars were too deep.

"He says the force of the explosion and the shrapnel are what make it so hard to improve the scars, but he seems to feel confident that I'll be happy with the result. I'm going back to New York over Christmas, have the surgery and spend a few days in the hospital."

"How long will you be there?"

"For two or three weeks after the surgery, depending on how it goes."

"Fantastic! I'm going home to Ireland for Christmas, which I'll regret the minute I get there. My sisters and nieces and nephews drive me crazy. But I'm coming back to New York for the New Year. Will you spend it with me?" She was touched that he would ask her.

"Yes, I will, unless you get a better date by then. You can cancel me if you do, if some little hottie crosses your path between now and the New Year."

"You're hottie enough for me." He laughed at her. "We can get shit-faced together, or go watch the ball drop in Times Square or something, on New Year's Eve. Where are you staying?"

"They have guest apartments for patients like me, from far away, who want to be 'discreet.' And you won't believe this, he and his partner are doing the first surgery for free, as a gift, to honor what happened to me."

"That really is amazing." Doug was happy for her. "I'm so glad it worked out. My friend raves about him."

"And he has a partner who does bodywork. He's going to clean up some of the worst scars for me. This is the best thing that has happened to me since the attack."

"Do you want to have dinner with me tomorrow night?" he offered. "I can't tonight. I have a date."

"I'd love to. And I'm too tired to go out tonight anyway. I just got back a few hours ago." She sounded sad again. "It's hard coming home to the apartment without my mom here. I keep thinking she'll walk out of her room, or I'll run into her in the kitchen. It still feels so unreal. Like it's a terrible joke or something, and she's going to walk in and tell me she was only kidding. But it's just me here, alone in the apartment."

"I felt like that after my father died too. Every time I went home to Dublin, I expected him to be there. I still do. Death is a hard concept to grasp, the idea that people disappear and vanish into thin air, and you never get to see them again."

"Yeah, that's how it is." He always understood. He was a fantastic friend. "Thank you for the referral. I really like both doctors. One is kind of movie star handsome and very smooth, and the other one, who does the bodywork, is this little teddy bear of a guy. They're both really nice, and I can't believe they're doing this for free."

"Some people want to put good energy back into the universe by doing good things. What happened to you and your mom was so wrong in so many ways. People feel helpless to fight it, so they do the best thing they can think of. It doesn't change what happened, but it's nice to know there are people like that in the world. It almost makes up for the others." It wouldn't bring her mother back, but it touched her, profoundly.

She got busy in her mother's closet again that night, and weeded out some things. She made piles of what she wanted to keep, and maybe use or wear herself. She made other piles of things to give away. She set a goal for herself, to get her mother's belongings put away by Christmas. Then she was going to streamline the apartment a little, move some things around, get rid of others, and make the apartment hers. There were a few things Véronique and her mother had never agreed on. For now, she still felt like she was living in her mother's apartment and not her own. She hadn't decided yet what to do with her mother's bedroom. She didn't want to sleep in it, and it made her too sad to take it apart and turn it into something else. But having it intact was part of what gave Véronique the feeling that her mother was going to walk through the front door any minute.

Dinner with Doug the next night was fun, as it always was. He'd been having a good time since she left, and had seen the young model again, and several others. He dated a lot of models. Véronique was one of the few who hadn't fallen for him. They had dinner at an Italian restaurant, and he told her the latest gossip from the fashion world. Hearing it made her miss it a little, but more and more she was feeling separate from it and as though the things that were so important to them meant absolutely nothing in the real world.

The day after they had dinner, she got to work on her mother's closets in earnest. She had gone through all her clothes by that night, and put them in neat piles. In the end, there was very little she wanted to keep, just a few sentimental things, and some pretty coats that Véronique used to borrow, and now they were hers. She went through Marie-Helene's jewelry and put it in the safe, since she knew she wouldn't wear it, and then she went through her desk, put photographs in boxes, piled her appointment books in a box, went through files, and papers. By dinnertime, Marie-Helene's desk was empty. Little by little, she was getting there. It felt disrespectful going through her things, but she wasn't coming back. Véronique was beginning to face that seven months after she'd died.

She spent the next month moving things around, replacing some curtains, getting rid of some furniture she didn't like. She was tired of her grandparents' antiques. She sent some to auction, moved some paintings around, and by November, the apartment looked different, younger, more cheerful. She had created an eclectic mix of old and new pieces. She had begun combing vintage stores and auction houses, and was excited when she brought things home. She wished she could have shown it to her mother. She might have liked it. Doug had gone back to New York by then, so she had no one to show it to, and enjoyed it herself. More and more, she was going out without her surgical mask. People stared at her sometimes, but she was learning to ignore it, and knowing that soon she was having the surgery helped. The damage to her face felt more temporary, like the results of an accident that were healing, instead of something that would stay that way forever.

She still didn't feel ready to see people she knew yet, and now she wanted to have the surgery in New York first, and maybe see some old friends after that.

Then finally, the inevitable happened. She had stopped worrying about it, and loved cruising around old shops in unfamiliar neighborhoods, looking for things for the apartment. It was early December. The Christmas decorations had gone up on the Champs Élysées and the avenue Montaigne. She loved walking around there sometimes when the lights came on at night. The city was getting ready for Christmas. She stopped at a grocery store on the way home, to pick up something to eat that night. She wasn't looking where she was going, and sometimes at night, her injured eye made it harder to judge distance and depth, and she collided with a woman leaving the store. She started to apologize and heard the woman gasp, and looked up and saw Stephanie, her agent. After months of avoiding everyone she knew, Véronique had run into, literally, the one person she wanted most to avoid. Stephanie was staring at her in shock. At first all she had seen were the scars, and then she realized who it was.

"Oh my God, Véronique, are you all right?" She sounded deeply concerned, and Véronique wanted to run away and hide, but it was too late. She couldn't escape. She didn't have the energy or even the desire to lie anymore.

"I'm fine," she said softly. "I'm sorry I bumped into you." She could see that Stephanie was staring at her face.

"Why didn't you tell me how bad it was?"

"I didn't know for a while myself or how long it would last. I still have some surgeries to get through." She no longer felt as though she had committed a crime, even though she wasn't beautiful anymore, and couldn't model. At first she had felt as though she had failed in some way. "I'm better now, but this is why I retired."

"I can see that now. But can't they do something about it? You can't just leave it like that," as though she had a choice, "they do such wonderful things these days. Have you seen a plastic surgeon?" As though the idea hadn't even occurred to her.

"Many times. I had twenty-six surgeries in six months." She said it more easily now. "I'm having another one in a few weeks. But it won't get much better than this. The scars will never completely go away. It's not exactly the right look for the cover of *Vogue*." There was a hint of irony in her voice. She didn't wake up wanting to cry about it anymore. The scars were fading a little, even before the surgery.

"Oh God, I'm sorry. You should have told me."

"Why? I retired, that's all they need to know. Models come and go."

"Not at your level. The big ones like you stay for a long time."

"Not like this," Véronique said simply. This was her reality, not evening gowns from Dior or Givenchy.

"What do the doctors say? Will it get better? Can they fix it?"

"Somewhat. Not enough for me to go back to work."

"Are you okay? Do you have a job?"

"I'm fine." She didn't owe her the details. "I didn't tell you because I didn't want everyone to feel sorry for me, or the press to chase me around. Apparently, some crap British tabloid did a story when I was in the hospital, but no one noticed it. I never saw it." She had been in a coma then, but a nurse had told her about it months later. "And my name didn't ring any bells on the casualty list. They talk about the people who died, but they don't say much about the injured."

"That's true. I'm glad I saw you. I get it now." Véronique noticed that she didn't suggest that they get together, or have lunch sometime. They weren't friends. Véronique had been a commodity she was selling. She was no longer saleable merchandise, so Stephanie was moving on. She could just imagine her telling people how Véronique looked, and about the scars on her face. She probably couldn't wait to tell them. She was a terrible gossip, and loved spreading bad news. Véronique was surprised to realize she didn't care. She couldn't worry anymore about what she would say.

"Stay in touch," Stephanie said unconvincingly. Véronique knew she wouldn't hear from her again, and there would be no calls before Fashion Week in March to ask if she'd walk in one of the shows. They both knew now that she wouldn't. "Well, take care," she said, as Véronique shook her head.

"Merry Christmas," Véronique said with a smile.

"You too. Call me after the next surgery and let me know if anything has changed." Véronique nodded, with no intention of doing it, and then walked away with a wave.

She felt oddly free after she'd seen her. She didn't need to hide anymore, or hope she didn't run into her. The worst had happened. Stephanie had seen her face, and would tell everyone what she looked like. And then she realized as she walked home that the worst had happened on March 22, when her mother and Cyril and thirty other people had died, and so many others had been injured. The rest, and what Stephanie said about her face, didn't matter at all.

Chapter 11

Véronique finished putting away her mother's things in December. Her desk had been cleared. Véronique was using her study now. Her mother's clothes were gone. Her books were still in the bookcase and would stay there. There were still photographs of Bill in the apartment, and she framed a number of the additional ones her mother had left her, and added them in the living room and her bedroom. They had new meaning for her now that she had met him. She loved the ones of her parents together and one of him holding her as a baby and beaming with pride.

Véronique noticed now how different the photographs were from the ones in his apartment, of him and his late wife standing side by side, looking awkward, with grim, ice-cold expressions. The joy and love Bill and Marie-Helene had shared was evident in every picture. Véronique couldn't help thinking whenever she saw them what a fool he had been to make the choice he had. He would have been happy with them. But he was well aware of it too, and had admitted it readily when she saw him.

She decided to get healthy and strong again after months of being inactive while she recovered. She swam almost every day, went for long walks, and rode her mother's bicycle in the Bois de Boulogne. She read all the books she'd wanted to read for the past few years, and hadn't had time to, and some old favorites.

She still didn't feel ready to contact people from her past. She'd lost contact with her school friends while she was modeling and working and traveling all the time. And her life had become too different from theirs. Some were jealous, and others had moved away, working or pursuing longer studies in other cities. At their ages, four years was a long time, and they had little in common now. She had landed in a very different world once she was modeling, and had led a more sophisticated life. She was back to basics now, but both fame and the trauma of the accident, and months in the hospital, had isolated her. Solitude was a habit now. And the biggest shock of all was losing her mother. She realized more than ever now how close they had been, and how empty her life was without her. Not having her support and the face she met people with now were obstacles she was still struggling to overcome.

She exchanged emails with a few of her mother's friends, but seeing them without her mother would only make Marie-Helene's absence more painful, and seemed too hard. Not wanting to intrude on her, they kept a discreet distance and they had their own problems, responsibilities, families, and busy lives. It made her regular contact with Doug even more precious to her.

She often went to movies in the afternoon. She got lost in the fantasy of the moment, and only went to funny movies that made her laugh, nothing too emotional or sad. She missed having someone to laugh with. And sometimes she turned on the TV in the apartment, just to hear voices and people in the house. Since the attack, she had led a solitary life. It was what she needed for now. She felt fragile after the trauma of what had happened in Brussels. Her computer was her main source of news and contact with the outside world, and she wrote to her father often. His responses were brief but warm and affectionate. He said he loved hearing from her, and he was leading an isolated life too, shut in at home, while his health continued to fail.

Now and then, she felt a wave of panic in a movie theater, or on the street, terrified that a bomb could explode near her. She read a lot about people who had survived trauma, and bought psychology books about PTSD. She realized that she was in transition between her old life, which had been shattered forever, and a new one, which hadn't taken shape yet. She still didn't know what she wanted to do about a job, but she wanted to get through her next two surgeries first before making any decisions. Her mind and her face and body were still engaged in the healing process, which for now was a full-time job.

She flew to New York on the twentieth of December. A light snow was falling when they took off from Paris. She would have loved to see it decorating the city, like lace on the lampposts. She had loved seeing it as a child.

It was bitter cold when she landed in New York. She was wearing an old raccoon coat of her mother's that she had kept, and a big matching fur hat.

She took a cab to the guest apartment they had assigned to her. It was perfect, just big enough to be comfortable. The bedroom was all done in pink chintz, the living room was a soft ivory, like their office. There were flowers to welcome her, a basket of fruit, soft drinks, champagne, wine, and a menu from the restaurant she could order meals from. She plugged in her computer and unpacked the night she arrived. She had brought mostly warm, comfortable clothes she would wear while recovering from the surgery. They had told her she would probably want to stay in for three to five days when she got home from the hospital, and both the pre- and post-op instructions were on the desk. Everything was meticulously organized.

She had an appointment with Dr. Talbot the next morning, and they did the necessary blood work. Her files had been sent from the hospital in Belgium, and both doctors had studied them carefully. They didn't want any surprises. They had a full body X-ray done, so they knew where the shrapnel was still lodged. They weren't going to try to remove any of it. They were only concerned with the surface, and the scars.

She met with Dr. Dennis after she saw Dr. Talbot. He gave her a warm welcome and a hug. Having a daughter the same age, he was fatherly toward her. He could see how excited she was about the surgery, and a little nervous. The only hospital she'd ever been in as a patient was the one in Brussels, and she was familiar with all their pre-op procedures. Here everything was different and unfamiliar, but it all went smoothly, and both doctors reassured her that it would be over quickly, and she'd be back in the apartment after a short stay in the hospital. They were going to keep her heavily sedated while in the hospital, and were going to keep her pain-free once back in the apartment. A nurse would check on her daily for the first few days, to watch for complications, but they didn't anticipate any problems. She had done very well after her surgeries in Belgium. They had read all her records, which had been sent to them. Aside from the effects of the attack, she was young and in good health.

Dr. Dennis chatted with her after he finished examining her body again. He had a map of all the scars, and had marked the ones he intended to work on, after Dr. Talbot worked on her face. They had worked as a team many times before, and had been partners for a dozen years. They'd met during Dr. Talbot's residency at Yale, and she gleaned from chatting with them that Dr. Dennis was married and had four children, and Dr. Talbot was divorced and currently single. Dr. Talbot was going to be on call on Christmas Eve and Day, so Dr. Dennis could be with his family. And Dr. Dennis was going to be on call on New Year's Eve, which he said he didn't care a whit about. He and his wife never went out on New Year's. One could tell that he was a family man. Dr. Talbot had two college-age children at UCLA, and neither of them was going to be with him at Christmas. He was meeting them in January for a long weekend to go skiing in Aspen. He had a house there.

"Maybe I'll be able to lure you to Africa with me one day," Dick Dennis said casually while Véronique dressed.

"Why Africa?" she said, as she pulled down her sweater and put on her boots. All of her tests and exams had checked out. She was surprisingly healthy and strong given what she'd been through nine months before. It was the blessing and advantage of youth. He was sure that many of the other victims hadn't fared as well.

"I spend three months in Angola every year," he explained to her, "at a children's hospital. Angola had twenty-seven years of civil war, which left them with over four million displaced people, incredible famine, and ten to fifteen million unexploded land mines. The damage to the population from those mines is heartbreaking. I got involved years ago with the HALO Trust. We're hoping to make Angola and several other countries free of land mines in the next few years. HALO has been working toward that for more than twenty years. I spend my three months there every year, operating on the children who are the victims of those mines. Many lose limbs or are severely disfigured. We round up the local children who've been injured, and provide free surgery and support services. The hospital is run by a small convent of nuns, and wonderful, dedicated nurses. They have medical teams who go through the area periodically. I do surgery there as a volunteer. You come back feeling as though you made some kind of difference. A three-year-old doesn't lose a leg, or a seven-year-old boy keeps his arm, or you try to repair what's left so they can function and maybe a little girl isn't disfigured. We see some awful stuff there. And the nurses and nuns are terrific.

"It's the only way I can do what I do here. You can only inject so much Botox, without feeling that you've wasted your medical school degree. Phillip is better at all that than I am. The work in Angola feeds my soul. Each of my kids has come out there at least once. Some like it better than others. My oldest son just started med school at Columbia. He's come out there with me a lot. The others aren't so keen on it. My wife hates it, but she's a good sport about letting me do what's important to me. She spends three months having dinner with her girlfriends, and I think she loves it." He laughed, and Véronique was fascinated by what he was saying. "Princess Diana was involved with HALO, and her son Prince Harry is now."

"I'd love to come out and see it sometime," she said spontaneously. "I've hardly been to Africa, just to Johannesburg once. I've worked just about everywhere else. South America, Asia, all over Europe, here in the States. I've never been anywhere else in Africa."

"I have a feeling you'd love it," he said warmly. His oldest son was twenty-four, and his next younger daughter was Véronique's age. "There's something very special about that part of the world. I fell in love with it when I was in college. I'm there roughly from February to May every year. I've been doing it for twenty years. I only stayed for two months when the kids were younger, or my wife would probably have divorced me. When they got to high school, I added the third month. I speak fluent Portuguese now, and some Kikongo and Umbundu, the other local languages. I'll tell you more about it if you'd be interested in going sometime." It was obvious how passionate he was about it, which touched her deeply. Her mind was full of her surgery the next day, and she was nervous about it, but she was intrigued by what he had told her and it sounded exciting.

She did a few errands after she left their office, and she called her father, hoping to see him. His nurse spoke to her, and said he wasn't well. He had a bad case of bronchitis and couldn't see anyone. She had written to him and told him about her surgery, and he had answered her and wished her luck. She asked the nurse to wish him a merry Christmas, and she said she would. His staff had been very responsive to her calls ever since she'd seen him, and she hoped to see him again while she was in New York, if his health permitted. She imagined him surrounded by his three children at Christmas. She was the unknown child in the shadows they knew nothing about and never would. It was an odd feeling. She was the secret he would take to his grave, as her mother had been too.

Doug called her on her cellphone that night from Ireland to wish her luck. He sounded a little drunk, said he had just come back from the pub with his brother, and that they were all driving him crazy but he was having a good time. He remembered to call her before her surgery. He'd been very good about staying in touch regularly, ever since she'd come back from Brussels. In the past, he had drifted off for months when they were busy, but now he made a point of calling her often, knowing how alone she was. He was her only friend at the moment, the only non-medical person who knew about her face other than Bernard, her father, Gabrielle, who had visited her once at the hospital, and her agent, whom she'd run into and never heard from again.

She had trouble sleeping that night, and got up at five. Since all her blood work had been done, she had to be at the hospital at six and the surgery was scheduled for eight. Both surgeons had said they would see her before the surgery. The hospital wasn't far from the apartment and their offices. She took a cab there at quarter to six. It was on the East River, and she arrived on time, and registered. She was taken to a private room, and the anesthesiologist came to see her and explained the procedure to her. It was all much fancier than anything she'd experienced in Belgium, but it was a private hospital, as opposed to a military one that was government run. The care there had been excellent, but it was more personalized here, with attention to every detail to contribute to her comfort.

They gave her something to relax her, and when Dr. Talbot and Dr. Dennis arrived, she was already sleepy and dozing off. They spoke to her for a few minutes and then left to scrub. She hardly noticed when the attendants came to put her on a gurney and roll her down the hall to the operating room. And once on the table, the room and bright lights were a familiar sight. It was cold, and they covered her with a heated blanket before they started. She was aware of both of her doctors in the room. A nurse put something in her IV, and within minutes the anesthesiologist told her to count backward from ten, and at nine she was unconscious.

The next thing she knew, she heard her name, and a nurse kept asking her questions she was too tired to answer. She was in the recovery room, and continued to doze. It seemed like a long time later when both doctors were standing next to her bed and telling her it had gone well.

"That's nice . . . thank you . . ." she said, and went back to sleep, and woke occasionally to say something to the nurse in French. They gave her some juice, and it was nighttime when she got back to her room. The nurse explained that they were giving her pain medication, but Véronique wasn't aware of any pain. She asked the nurse if there had been a second bomb and if her mother was all right. The nurse said that both her doctors had come to see her again while she was asleep. She never answered her about the bomb and her mother. When they helped her to the bathroom a while later, she asked how Cyril was, and the nurse said he was fine. They were used to post-op patients, and she was getting strong medications. Her face was heavily bandaged, and she slept through the night and woke in the morning. It was snowing outside, and there was a foot of snow on the windowsill. Her mouth felt like cotton from the anesthesia. Dr. Talbot came to see her at eight A.M. and she was starting to come out of the fog.

"It looks like we're going to have a white Christmas for you." He smiled at her. It had taken him twenty minutes to get from his office a few blocks away on slippery streets. "How are you feeling, Véronique?"

"Tired, but okay." She didn't like the sensation of her face bandaged again. It felt suffocating and brought back bad memories, but she wasn't in pain.

"You just spend the next few days sleeping." There were bandages on her legs and arms too, from Dr. Dennis's work, and a large bandage on her stomach. "We did some good work yesterday," he said, looking pleased. "I think we'll all be happy with it. Everything went fine."

She spent the next two days more asleep than awake, with the medications they were giving her, and both doctors came to see her on Christmas morning. They had lightened the dose of pain medication, and she was more alert. There was even more snow on the windowsill. The city was nearly shut down after a blizzard. She had slept through all of it.

"How are you feeling?" Dr. Talbot asked her, as Dr. Dennis checked the bandages on her legs and was satisfied. She had barely moved out of bed in three days except to go to the bathroom, and most of the time she had thought she was in Belgium. She knew where she was now. It was Christmas morning. "Would you like to go back to the apartment today?" Dr. Talbot asked her. There was no reason to keep her in the hospital. Where she felt most comfortable was really up to her.

"Yes," she said, her voice a croak from not speaking much for three days, and the anesthetic.

"We'll have a car pick you up this afternoon, and a nurse will be with you tonight and tomorrow after you go home. After that you should be okay on your own." She realized then that Dr. Dennis had come in specially to see her, even though he wasn't on duty on Christmas Day. But his children were old enough to manage without him for an hour. In fact, they all had plans, and were going to be coming and going all day.

Both doctors signed the release papers before they left, and she lay awake in her bed, totally lucid for the first time in three days. The days after the surgery had just slipped by her. The room was quiet and the nurses had been attentive. There was nothing much for them to do except check that she hadn't pulled off any of her bandages, but she hadn't moved.

A nurse helped her dress at four o'clock, and a nurse's aide wheeled her downstairs, and the doorman helped her from the wheelchair into the car her doctors had sent. Everything was covered in snow, and the city looked beautiful as they drove the short distance to the apartment. The nurse was waiting for her in the lobby and helped her upstairs, settled her in the big comfortable bed, and asked if she wanted the TV turned on, but she didn't. She had completely missed Christmas, and she was glad she had. She lay in the bed thinking about her mother, and the beautiful Christmases they had shared. She hadn't put up a tree since she was leaving, and couldn't have borne the thought of decorating one without her.

The nurse was very quiet, and sat in the living room. She came to check on Véronique every half hour or so. She had a light meal sent in of chicken, rice, and chicken soup, but Véronique ate very little. She was asleep by nine o'clock, and as she drifted off, she was glad that she had missed Christmas without her mother. It had been the perfect way to get through it, under heavy sedation. The nurse turned off the light, and Véronique didn't stir until morning.

When she woke up the day after Christmas, she said she didn't need any pain medication. The nurse helped her sponge off around the bandages, and then helped her dress. She put on jeans and a gray sweatshirt and fuzzy slippers. She turned on the TV, and the nurse served her the scrambled eggs she'd ordered. She left at six o'clock, and Véronique was on her own, four days post-op, with nurses who would come twice a day to check her bandages. Dr. Talbot called before dinnertime to see how she was feeling.

"Fine, except I feel like I've been on a two-week drunk," she said, slightly embarrassed. Once she was out of the coma, they hadn't sedated her as heavily in Brussels, except for her more serious surgeries.

"It's only been four days," he corrected her, "and that's the best way to do it. You didn't miss anything, except a big snowstorm."

"Can I go out?" It looked so pretty she wanted to go out and make a snowball.

"Better not to. You don't want to fall and bump anything. In a few days the snow will be gone. You can go out then. Dick will be upset if you mess up any of his handiwork. I'll come and see you tomorrow, but the nurses have been reporting that you're doing well. No pain?"

"None. My face tingles a little, but it doesn't hurt."

"That's perfect. Just take it easy and watch movies."

She felt very lazy, but she was tired, and she was still sleeping a lot. She couldn't wait to get all the drugs out of her system. It was a sensation she didn't like, and reminded her of all her surgeries in Belgium.

She called her father that afternoon, and this time he was awake, and well enough to talk to her. He coughed a lot on the phone, but he seemed in good spirits.

"How did the surgery go?" he asked her immediately. "I've been worried about you."

"Okay, I think. I've just been sleeping for the past four days. I don't even know what happened, except that I look like a mummy again. I'm all bandaged up."

"Just rest. The city has been shut down anyway, with all the snow."

"I wanted to go out and make snowballs, but the doctor won't let me." She sounded like a little girl and he laughed.

"They won't let me go out and make snowballs either. You'll have to come for another visit when we're both feeling better. I've got this damn cough. I don't know how I got it. Were you all right on Christmas?" He had been concerned about her, on her first Christmas without her mother.

"I slept through it."

"Maybe that's for the best," he said wistfully. She thought so too.

They talked for a few more minutes, and then he started coughing more heavily, so they hung up, and before they did, she said, "Merry Christmas, Papa," and he laughed and sounded pleased.

"I've waited a long time to hear that. Thank you. Merry Christmas to you too, darling girl. I hope you have a wonderful year ahead, much better than the last one."

"Yeah, I hope so too." It couldn't have been much worse, and then they hung up, and she was glad she had spoken to him. He didn't sound well. His cough sounded awful, but he said he didn't have pneumonia when she asked.

It had turned out to be a perfectly tolerable Christmas. Doug was coming back to New York from Ireland in three days, and they were going to spend New Year's Eve together since he didn't have a date. She was looking forward to seeing him. He was busy with his family and she hadn't heard from him again from Dublin. She had brought a short silver dress to wear that a designer had given her after a shoot. Doug said he'd bring champagne. They were going to stay at the apartment, and watch old movies on TV. It sounded like a perfect New Year's Eve to her, and she was glad she had done the surgery. Now all they needed to do was see the results. So far, her doctors had taken extraordinary care of her. It had been a first-class experience, nothing like the military hospital in Brussels. She felt like a queen, and it was free.

Doug arrived promptly at nine on New Year's Eve, and his eyes grew wide when he saw her in her silver dress, and high heels to match. You could see her bandages, but you could see her legs too, and the effect was a knockout. He looked impressed.

"Hello, Tin Man, I love you!" he said in a heavy brogue. It bothered her more that half her face was bandaged again, which brought back bad memories. She'd had nightmares every night since the surgery. But she was happy to see him. He was carrying a bottle of champagne, opened it, poured two glasses and handed her one, and sat down next to her on the couch in her borrowed apartment. "Fancy digs," he said, glancing around, impressed. It looked like a top-notch five-star hotel. She had ordered dinner for them from the catering service. She had ordered a steak for him and chicken for herself. He was relaxed and happy after his trip to Ireland.

"So how was it?" she asked, as they sipped the champagne.

"Fantastic. My family is crazy. We were all squashed into my mother's tiny apartment, and hung out at the local pub at every opportunity. Even old ladies go there. My older brother drinks too much, but he's a great guy. He has a terrible wife, though. We've all hated her for years. And my sister Nuala who's a nun got to spend Christmas with us. I forget how much I love being back there when I'm here. My mother lives for when we're all at home together. She puts up with all of us, and cooks for an army, all the traditional Irish dishes. I'm glad I went. It all seems like too much trouble, until I get there, and then I'm happy to be back in Ireland. How were you here?" he asked, concerned.

"I slept my way through the holidays. They kept me drugged up, but now I feel fine."

The food arrived at nine-thirty, and Doug enjoyed his steak. Véronique had chicken and only picked at her meal. She wasn't hungry after all the drugs she'd been taking, but she'd already been out by then, and had gone walking in the park in the snow. She had watched the children playing, and sliding down the hills wearing garbage bags tied around them. She wanted to try it, but was afraid to bang up her legs. Both doctors were pleased with how she'd come through the surgery, and said she could go home in two weeks. Her bandages were due to come off a few days before she left.

They talked while they ate, and she told him about Dr. Dennis's work with children in Africa. "He invited me to come out and visit. I'm thinking about going in March after the next surgery, or April. It sounds amazing."

"I've been to Kenya and Zimbabwe. I loved it. There are some beautiful places. He must be a good man if he does that and works for free for three months every year."

"I think so too. He lights up when he talks about the kids. The hospital is run by nuns. He said I can stay in the convent if I go."

"Please don't sign up while you're there. I still can't believe my sister did. She used to date every boy in the parish, and then she joined an order, took her vows, and that was it. My mother was thrilled. If we'd all become priests and nuns, she'd have loved it. I moved to New York to get away from my family. But once a year they're great." He looked happy and relaxed.

They had the TV on in the background so they could see the ball in Times Square. It was going to be the highlight of their evening. She was grateful he was spending it with her. She had gone to a movie one afternoon, and the Metropolitan Museum, but she didn't have anything to do. After ten days in New York, she was ready to go home, but she had to wait for the removal of her bandages. She was anxious to see the results of the surgery. They warned her that her face would be a little pink for a while, but the scars were supposed to be smoother and lighter.

"This is all your doing, you know. If you hadn't given me Dr. Talbot's name, I'd be in Brussels getting patched up with the soldiers."

"I'm glad you called him. I hope they did a good job. He did on my friend. She's happy and back at work." They knew that wasn't going to happen to Véronique, her modeling days were over, but any improvement was welcome. She told him about running into Stephanie in Paris before Christmas, and he groaned, which was her feeling about it too. "She's such a gossip and a drama queen, God knows what she's telling people. I was worried about it at first, but in the end, I figured what the hell. I can't stop her from talking. And I'm better now." Her spirits were better. He had noticed it. She seemed more confident, and never wore the surgical mask anymore. She went out with the scars on her face showing, even before her recent surgery.

Doug finished off the champagne while they waited for the ball to drop. They had talked about going to Times Square to see it, but she didn't want to get jostled in the crowd, and have someone bump her, and it was freezing out so they were happy to watch it on TV. She had stopped at one glass of champagne and was sober. He was slightly drunk, but not too much so. It just made him funny, and not obnoxious. And even when he drank a lot, he was always a happy drunk.

Then finally, it was midnight and the ball dropped with all the fanfare and horn blowing. He kissed her chastely on the mouth, and half an hour later, he got up to go.

"Late night date?" she teased him.

"No, jet lag. If I stay any longer, you'll have to let me sleep on the couch." He'd done that before at her apartment, but she agreed that he should go while he was still mobile.

"Thank you for making it a nice New Year's Eve for me," she thanked him when he left. He hugged her gently, so he didn't hurt anything. She seemed so fragile to him now.

"You make it nice for me too," he said. "One of these days, we'll meet the loves of our lives, and we won't be doing this anymore."

"I can't imagine that scenario for me now," she said. "The guy would have to be blind."

"No. He just has to love you, and be good to you, or I'll kick his ass." She had become like a little sister that he wanted to protect from all the evils in the world. She had already run into enough of them for a lifetime. "When you get all this medical shit behind you, you'll run into the right guy one of these days. At twenty-three, you're not exactly an old maid yet. I'm not worried about you." But he hoped that she didn't let the scars on her face keep her from letting love into her life. It would be terrible if she shut herself away. "We'll go dancing sometime," he promised. He knew she loved to dance. She smiled thinking about it, and a few minutes later he left, back out in the freezing cold. She was happy they had stayed home.

It had been a warm, cozy evening, and he was a good friend. She couldn't imagine a man being in her life again. Poor Cyril was a dim memory now, although she still thought of him. She had spent last New Year's Eve with him at a fabulous black-tie party in Monte Carlo. They had flown down for the night. That all seemed so long ago now. It was part of another life. One she couldn't imagine having again. The bomb at Zaventem had taken care of that.

Chapter 12

Véronique spent a quiet New Year's Day reading and watching TV. She had adjusted to her damaged right eye and reduced vision, and she read a great deal. She went for a walk in the park, all bundled up, and called her father when she got home. She offered to visit him, but he admitted that he was tired and not feeling well. He sounded as though his cough had gotten worse.

"How are you feeling since the surgery?" he asked. For someone who had been an absentee father for her entire life, since they had reconnected, he had made himself accessible to her whenever she called. He was concerned about her and all that she was facing. He knew she no longer had her mother to watch over her, so he felt it was his turn now, even at this late date. He owed at least that to Marie-Helene, and knew how she adored their child. Losing her had been hard for Véronique, harder than her scars, and the career she had lost.

"I feel fine. I want to see how it looks. They keep telling me that it won't be a huge improvement, just a slight one with each surgery, but eventually it won't look quite as shocking as it does now. It is what it is. It won't ever go away completely," nor would the trauma of what she'd been through. She knew that too, and she got anxious whenever she was in crowds. The airports in Paris and New York had been terrifying for her, but she had managed it anyway. She didn't want it to stop her life, and she was willing to face her demons. The likelihood of anything like it ever happening to her again was beyond remote. She and Dr. Verbier had talked a lot about that. But the memories were still vivid. It had only been nine months since the attack.

"I want you to come and visit me again," her father said warmly, but he sounded exhausted. It had taken him two days to recover from their long visit. "Come and see me when the bandages come off. I'll have gotten rid of this damn cough by then."

"Don't go outside, Papa," she warned him, savoring the word. She loved saying it. It was like a gift he had given her. "It's bitter cold."

"Don't worry, I'm not going anywhere. Although the snow looks lovely from my windows. I used to love the snow in Paris when I went to visit your mother. It's such a beautiful city."

"It is." She missed it. New York was an unfamiliar place, even though she had worked there often, but she couldn't imagine living there. It was exciting, but everything about it seemed hard and cold to her. It had none of the charm of Paris.

They talked for a while, until his coughing fits stopped him. It was a deep wracking cough that worried her.

"Chip is coming to see me today." He was her half-brother. He was her father's oldest child and only son. He was fifty-three years old, thirty years older than Véronique. He had two younger sisters, who were in their forties. They could have been her parents.

"You sound tired, Papa," Véronique said gently, "you should rest."

"I will, I'm going to take a nap before he comes. You take care of yourself too. Do what the doctors tell you."

"I do. I've been very careful not to bump anything after the surgery." The skin was very thin now on her arms and legs since her injuries. "A nurse comes to check the dressings every day."

"Be careful you don't fall," he warned her. "It must be icy and slippery outside." He was right. She had almost slipped a few times when she'd gone for a walk.

"I am careful. I'll come and see you soon. I'll call you tomorrow to see how you are." And then she added, "I love you," in her gentle voice. Hearing it brought tears to his eyes. He had missed so much with her. Her entire life. And she sounded so much like her mother. They had the same voice.

"I love you too. I hope you know that," he said in a fatherly way.

"Now I do."

"I always did, and your mother. Be careful of the choices you make. We regret our mistakes all our lives." She didn't know what to say to him, to comfort him. It was clear to her that he regretted not staying with Marie-Helene and their child. It was too late now, but at least they had found each other and finally met, at the right time for both of them. His wife was no longer there, and she was grateful to have a father, now that she had lost her mother. He was trying to offer Véronique some support in her absence.

"It turned out all right," she said softly. "Maman and I were happy together. She had a good life," she tried to reassure him. There was no point for him to torture himself now, he was old and sick. Véronique had a forgiving nature, her mother had taught her that, and had been a shining example of it in her own life. She had been a role model for Véronique in so many ways.

"I'll talk to you soon," he said, his voice fading, and a minute later, they both hung up. She thought about him for the rest of the day, and what he'd said.

She went to bed early that night, after watching a movie. She knew Doug was having dinner with a girl he'd met on the plane coming back from Ireland. She woke up in the morning, feeling fresh and energized, when the nurse came to change her dressings. Véronique had just woken up, and the nurse put *The New York Times* on the table next to her, and Véronique went to make a cup of coffee. The nurse left after she'd checked the bandages, and then Véronique sat down with her coffee and the paper.

A headline on the front page stopped her in her tracks. It was a photograph of her father when he was younger, and the headline read, SENATOR WILLIAM HAYES DEAD AT 83. BELOVED ELDER STATESMAN DIED OF PNEUMONIA AT HIS HOME. It said he had passed away the previous afternoon, and she realized with an aching heart that he must have died not long after she spoke to him. She was so glad she had called him. Tears slid down her face as she read the article, about his many political victories, the laws he had helped to pass, the vice presidential candidacy that had failed. It said he was survived by his three children, Charles Hayes, who was currently running for a congressional seat, Adele Hayes Harriman, and Elizabeth

Hayes Sutton, and seven grandchildren. He had been married to the late Florence Astor Hayes for fifty-six years, and she had passed away the previous year. The article said he had retired shortly after, and had been suffering from ill health for several years. Mrs. Hayes had died of Alzheimer's.

They mentioned the senator's many philanthropic activities. He was well known for his generous donations, as was his wife. It listed the numerous Senate subcommittees he'd been on, the important changes he had initiated, and said that he was one of the most respected and beloved members of the Senate. Nowhere did it mention Véronique or her mother of course. They were the best-guarded secrets of his life, that he had taken to his grave. But everything said about him spoke of a noble life, dedicated to improving conditions for others.

He had been instrumental in many of the anti-poverty programs, and she found herself wondering if he and her mother had been right to protect him from even a hint of scandal. The obituary would have read differently if a mistress in Paris and a love child had been disclosed, or a nasty divorce for those reasons. The decision not to expose him to that had been made jointly. Yet, from what he said, it was clear to Véronique that he regretted that decision in the end. She would miss him no less now than if he had been her legitimate father. The connection had been made, and even though only recent, their bond was strong. He had arrived in time to be a huge loss to her. She sat crying, thinking of everything they had said the day before. Most of all, he had told her he loved her, and always had, and her mother, and she believed him. She truly was an orphan now, and she had no one to share the loss with. She knew his death would have broken her mother's heart, and maybe they were together now. She hoped so. His fifty-six-year marriage to Florence Astor had been an empty one, and their last years together couldn't have been easy either if she had Alzheimer's. It was Marie-Helene he spoke of as the love of his life.

The article said that the funeral mass would be in four days at Saint Patrick's Cathedral, and was open to the public. Burial would be private for family only. A rosary was to be said at the cathedral the night before.

She sat for hours, staring into space, thinking of him, shocked that he had slipped away so quickly, and she hadn't seen him again. She cherished the short time they had shared, and their exchanges. She cried every time she thought of him and their conversation the day before. She wondered if he had sensed it was the end. He had been so clear and so insistent when he said he loved her.

She was still sitting on the couch with the newspaper in her hand when Doug called her. He had just seen it in the paper.

"Oh my God, Véro, I'm so sorry. He has such an impressive background. When did you last see him?"

"Not since the last time I was here, when I came to meet him. But we've talked a lot on the phone, I talked to him yesterday and he told me he loved me." She was crying. "I'm an orphan now, for real." She sobbed as she said it, and he felt terrible for her. "He told me he was sorry he didn't stay with my mother, but maybe they were right. It would have been a huge scandal. I don't know if they should have braved it or not," but they hadn't, for whatever reason. "My mother didn't want to hurt his political future. I guess he had his eye on the presidency, but he never ran for president, just vice president, and lost anyway."

"He did an awful lot of great stuff, if you read the article in the *Times*. He championed all the anti-poverty programs, and was a huge philanthropist personally. You really have to admire him for who he was. That's quite a legacy to have someone like him as your father."

"I know. I just wish I'd had more time with him, even now as an adult. I was fine with just my mom growing up, although it would have been nice to have him with us. But with my mom gone, he's been very attentive and engaged, and now he's gone too." She'd really had a terrible year, losing both her parents, and her father so soon after he came into her life. "It's probably stupid, but I'm going to go to the funeral. It's open to the public, so I won't embarrass anyone. No one will even know I'm there, but I want to be there for him. I won't bother anyone, or approach his kids. I think my mother would have wanted me to go. He is my father after all, even if no one knows."

"It's going to be mobbed. Everyone admired and loved him. But I think you should go, if it's not too hard for you." She'd been through enough without adding more unnecessary trauma, but maybe it would give her some kind of comfort and closure to be there.

"I wish I could go with you," he said. "I have a big shoot on Friday for *Harper's Bazaar*."

"I'll be okay," she said, calming down a little. The funeral gave her something to focus on. "The nurse took some of the bandages off my face today, and I just have gauze and tape now, so I won't look like a mummy in a horror movie if I go, but I would have gone that way anyway, if I had to." He knew she would have. She had shown nothing but guts and courage in the past ten months. He didn't doubt that for a moment.

They talked for a few more minutes after that, and she left the apartment immediately after, bundled up against the cold. She wanted to find something appropriate to wear to her father's funeral. They had buried her mother quietly with a private service that only she and her mother's law partner had attended. This time, she wanted to do her father proud, even if no one in the crowd knew who she was, and she was a secret from everyone who knew him. She was his daughter to her core, and she was going to look it, and represent herself and her mother.

She took a cab to Bergdorf, and began a serious search for something appropriate to wear. She knew all the designers well, and who was most likely to have what she needed, and by six o'clock she had found all of it. She was going to be the most quietly elegant woman at the funeral, lost among thousands of strangers and members of the public. She found a beautiful black wool Balenciaga coat from their couture collection, reminiscent of the clothes Audrey Hepburn had worn, and Jacqueline Kennedy. She hadn't brought anything appropriate with her, and didn't own anything quite that grown up, but this was going to be one of the most adult events in her life, and she wanted him to be proud of her, wherever he was now. She found a simple black wool Dior dress to go under it. She was going to wear opaque black stockings so the gauze bandages on her legs didn't show, and very high-heeled black suede Manolo Blahnik pumps, and a plain black alligator handbag her mother would have loved. And a pair of short black kid gloves.

The last piece she needed she knew would be more difficult, but she didn't want to go bareheaded with a large square of gauze on her cheek as the first thing one noticed about her. She wasn't going to wear a surgical mask again. And after trying on every black hat in the store, she found the perfect one by Gucci. It was black felt with a very large brim and a small crown, that fit her perfectly. The brim was large but not ridiculously so. It was very glamorous in a quiet way, and you had to be as tall as she was to pull it off. She tilted it just slightly, as she would have for a cover shoot. It gave it an extra something, and by tilting it infinitesimally, it almost concealed the bandage on her face, though not entirely, just enough, and drew attention to the left side of her face. The injured right side was slightly in shadow, and somewhat concealed by the hat, and made her look elegant and mysterious. It was perfect with the coat and what she'd bought. It all fit perfectly, and she tried it on again when she got home, and was satisfied. She knew what suited her and how to wear it. She would be noticeable in the best possible way, as an elegant young woman, impeccably and appropriately dressed for the occasion. She sensed that both of her parents would have been proud of her if they could see her, and she hoped they could. She looked like a model again, worthy of the cover of *Vogue*.

She spent the next three days thinking of him, and went to a nearby church to light a candle for him. On Friday, she dressed carefully. She wore a minimum of eye makeup, perfectly applied and barely noticeable, and dressed in what she'd bought. She put the hat on with great care, at just the right angle, and the mirror told her that she had arrived at the right effect, when she left with the car and driver she had hired for the occasion. She arrived an hour before the service, to be sure she would find a seat in the church. People were quietly lined up to pay their respects. Many had gone to the rosary the night before, but she didn't. She found a seat more easily than she'd expected to. With one glance at her, one of the ushers, chosen from his senatorial staff, led her to a pew about a dozen rows behind the family. She looked like someone important who belonged there, and she sat praying quietly, her eyes drifting to the mahogany casket covered with a blanket of lily of the valley and white phalaenopsis orchids. The church was filled to bursting, and she stood with everyone else when the family filed in, with her half-brother, Charles, in the lead alone, his three teenage sons behind him, and Véronique's half-sisters behind them, one with her husband and twin sons, and the other with her husband and a boy and a girl. Their husbands were both bankers, and all of them wore black suits, and the women in black dresses with plain black coats over them. But none had the striking look of Bill's youngest child, in her exquisite hat and coat. They all appeared sober and very sad.

The sermon and eulogy were predictably impressive and respectful. Three of his senatorial colleagues spoke about how important Bill Hayes had been to the country and to them. Charles spoke on behalf of the family, with a moving eulogy to honor his father. Véronique couldn't help noticing that Bill's oldest daughter looked strikingly like her. They had the same tall, slim bodies and similar faces, only Adele was blond. Elizabeth was shorter, and looked more like her mother and had dark hair. Adele had worn a small black fur hat, and Elizabeth was wearing a black lace mantilla that had been her mother's and she had worn to her funeral the previous year. This was a heavy double loss for all of them, just as it was for Véronique

172

in different circumstances. But the loss of both parents was a hard blow. And all of Bill Hayes's children had lost their mother in the past year too.

Véronique was seated on the aisle, and lined up to take Communion. She advanced slowly with the line, and stood inches away from her half-brother, as she waited near the front of the line, and he sat on the aisle in the first pew. Instinctively, he turned to look at her. She was a beautiful woman. He could barely see the bandage on her cheek with the tilt of her hat, but something about her held his attention as he stared at her. There was something so familiar about her, the way she stood and moved, and even her face, and she was so beautiful that he would have noticed her anyway. Their eyes met for an instant, and everything she felt for her father was in them, and it struck him. He watched as she moved forward to take Communion, and on her way back down the aisle, he saw the exquisite left half of her face, more exposed than the other side under her hat, and a moment later, she had disappeared into the crowd, and into the pew where she was sitting.

At the end of the mass, she whispered, "Goodbye, Papa," and threaded her way through the crowd with tears running down her cheeks. Charles saw the hat disappear toward the doors of the church, and then she was gone. She slipped into the car after walking down the steps. Several photographers took her photograph, because she looked so elegant and striking, and she hoped they didn't recognize her. She slipped on dark glasses, and once in the car, it pulled away to take her back to the apartment, where she carefully took off her hat and coat, and sat down in the black dress to read the funeral program again. There was a beautiful photograph of her father on the cover, and the music during the service had been magnificent with the cathedral organ. They had played Beethoven's "Ode to Joy" at the end, and the Ave Maria and "Amazing Grace" during the service, which had reduced Véronique to tears. Compared to her mother's simple graveside service, her father's funeral was all pomp and ceremony, as suited his stature as a respected senator.

After the long, emotional day, she wasn't hungry and made herself some chicken broth and toast for dinner. She was at the table in her nightgown, after she took her funeral clothes off, when the phone rang, and she assumed it would be Doug, asking her how it had gone. She felt drained and didn't want to speak to anyone, even Doug. She wasn't going to answer, but the ringing was persistent, and she finally answered the phone, it was from a blocked number. A deep male voice spoke when she answered it.

"Miss Vincent?"

"Yes."

He sounded serious and somewhat cautious, and the voice was vaguely familiar but she couldn't place it.

"This is Charles Hayes, William Hayes's son," he said, as her heart skipped a beat. She couldn't imagine why he was calling her. He sounded so official, she was worried that he was going to threaten her in some way, and tell her not to contact any of them, which she wouldn't have anyway. Her mother had been extremely careful and respectful too. "If convenient for you, I'd like to make an appointment to see you. It was one of my father's last wishes, on the day he died." She remembered that he said Chip was coming to see him. She wondered what her father had said to him about her. "Would it be possible for us to meet?" he asked, and she was so stunned she didn't speak for a minute, and then rushed to answer him.

"Yes, of course. The service was beautiful. Everything about it, the music, the flowers, the tributes. What you said was very moving."

"He was an amazing man, and a wonderful father. We were very lucky," he said. Luckier than she was, to only have had him for such a short time. "Would tomorrow be convenient for you?"

"Yes." She had nothing to do, and even if she did, she would have seen him anyway. This was important, she wanted to know what it was about, and didn't want to ask him on the phone. He suggested they meet at the Carlyle, which was convenient for both of them.

"At five o'clock?" he suggested.

"That's fine." He hadn't mentioned his sisters, and she wondered if they were coming too. She couldn't tell if this was going to be a meeting to warn her off and get rid of her, or embrace her as their long-lost sister, with open arms. She couldn't guess from anything he said. She wondered if she was walking into some kind of trap, but wanted to go anyway.

"Thank you," he said politely, "this meeting was important to my father. He made that very clear to me."

"I'm so sorry. I know he wasn't well, but I didn't expect this, not so soon anyway."

"Neither did we. It's been a shock to all of us. I wish he could have lived to a hundred."

"So do I," she said softly.

"See you tomorrow at five," he said before he hung up, and Véronique spent the rest of the night worrying about why he wanted to meet her and what he would say. What if he threatened her? But he was so polite and well brought up, that was hard to imagine. He seemed very conservative and formal when she saw him at the funeral. Whatever he said or did, there was no question in her mind. She had to go, even if for no other reason than to honor their father. They had him in common, even if they had nothing else, and never saw each other again after the meeting.

Chapter 13

Véronique arrived at the Bemelmans Bar at the Carlyle on the dot of five. She wore her black Balenciaga coat again, with simple black slacks and a black sweater, and black flats. She didn't feel up to wearing color. The bandage on her face showed clearly without her hat, but it looked better than what was under it. She had worn her hair pulled back in a bun. She looked younger than she had the day before, and less glamorous, but she still looked beautiful and elegant. She was a striking woman no matter what she wore.

Charles Hayes was already at a quiet corner table, waiting for her, and stood up the moment she walked in. She recognized him too and made her way toward him, with a small nervous smile, not sure what she was in for. He invited her to sit down, never taking his eyes off her.

"I saw you yesterday," he said immediately, "or I thought it was you. You looked very elegant and very French, and you look a lot like my sister and paternal grandmother, and my dad. I hope I didn't

upset you by calling yesterday. My father took me into his confidence the day he died. I never knew anything about you or your
mother, or even suspected. No one did. I don't think he wanted to
take a secret like that with him, and I'm the executor of his estate,
so questions would have surfaced eventually, and I think he wanted
me to hear it from him." Véronique nodded and listened as he went
on. He didn't seem angry at her so far, and wasn't treating her as an
intruder. They shared a secret now, which potentially could make
them allies, depending on how he viewed it, or enemies if he chose.
But he didn't seem hostile. He was very polite, and had kind eyes.

"My parents had a difficult marriage. We all figured that out once
we grew up. They weren't well suited to each other. My mother was
very distant, even with her children. My father was a much warmer
person and he made up for it. But I never suspected that there was
another woman or a child, until he told me a few days ago. He told
me that he loved your mother very much, and that you had been in
touch with him recently, and he saw you. He spoke very highly of
her." He smiled at Véronique. This was a difficult meeting for him
too, meeting his father's love child and talking about his mistress.
"Oddly enough, my mother hated politics, and his political career,
she always did. And yet he stayed with her. But he told me he didn't
want the scandal that it would have caused if he got divorced, particularly if the circumstances surrounding you and your mother
came to light. Americans are puritans, and hypocrites sometimes. It
wouldn't have gone well with his constituents, or played well in the
press, even though lots of politicians have affairs and children out
of wedlock. Americans expect their political leaders to be above re-
proach. I'm getting a taste of that myself. I'm in the midst of a di-

vorce. My father encouraged me to do it, and not spend the rest of my life unhappy with the wrong person. He made it very clear to me the other day that he regretted not staying with your mother, and risking the fallout of it publicly. He said she left him so she wouldn't spoil his political chances, which was certainly noble of her. She must have been a very good woman, and she never made trouble for my father, nor did you." Charles smiled at her. "She was an honorable woman, and he was a good man. He wanted me to meet you, and we are brother and sister after all. I would have known about you anyway, because I'm the executor of his will, and there's a provision in it for you." She looked shocked when he said it. "He wanted to be sure that you'll be all right, with your mother gone and after what happened in Brussels." So he knew all that too.

She was shocked to hear about the money. She hadn't expected that, since he had provided for her very handsomely when he and Marie-Helene parted.

"Do your sisters know about me?" she asked, curious, and he shook his head, with a grave expression. He was a serious-looking man, with gray at his temples.

"My father was specific about that too. He left it up to me after he was gone, but he didn't think they should. He wanted me to hear it from him directly, which is why he told me that day. I think it's why he asked me to come over. He died only a few hours later, while he was having a nap after I left. My sisters are both very traditional and conservative. They're married. Their husbands are bankers. I don't think it would ever occur to them that our father would have an affair, or another child. They prefer to believe the illusion of our parents' marriage. I don't think they'd want to know the truth, and they might react badly to it. I have more realistic ideas. My own marriage was a disaster, and I know what it feels like to be trapped in a loveless marriage. I don't blame my father for his involvement with your mother, or the turn it took. In a way I envy him to be able to say so clearly that she was the love of his life, and truly mean it. He had no regrets about her, only about their parting and not staying together. He said he regretted that deeply, and apparently, he missed your entire childhood and was sorry about that too."

"He said that to me too," she said softly.

"I don't think my sisters are open-minded enough to understand that. They have the self-satisfied attitudes of people who are content in their marriages. They've been critical of me for getting divorced, and would have been of my father, I suspect. He thought so too. There's not much to be served in forcing the point with them now, with him gone. If he were still alive, it might be different, so that you could be accepted openly. But now, with him gone, there's not much in it for you. He set up the bequest for you confidentially, in such a way that they'll be unaware of it, and I'm under the obligation to follow his wishes and keep it confidential, as his executor. So there's no cause for jealousy either, and there's more than enough for everyone.

"Maybe I'll see it differently with my sisters later, and it's up to you ultimately. You have a right to contact them if you want to. But given the hard line they've taken with me, I would warn you to be cautious with them. I can help you on that front, if you want me to, maybe after the shock of his death has worn off. But what I wanted to do today was meet you and hold a hand out to you as your brother, and share with you the loss of our wonderful father. I'm here to help you in any way I can."

Tears filled her eyes before she could answer him, and not knowing what else to do, she hugged him, and he held her. He felt sorry for her. He had heard all about the Brussels attack from their father, and about all that she had lost, and the severe injuries she'd sustained. He thought she was still beautiful, but the large square of gauze on her face suggested that all was not entirely well yet, and his father had said as much to him, that she had been severely disfigured in the explosion, as well as losing her mother. But he thought she was still spectacular looking, whatever was under the gauze.

"Thank you, Charles," she said, when she let go of him.

"Call me Chip." He smiled at her. "So now you have a big brother." He realized that she could have been his daughter. She was barely older than his sons. "I'd like you to meet my boys someday, your nephews." He smiled at her. He understood better now why his father had encouraged him to get divorced, despite his own political ambitions, rather than stay with a woman he no longer loved. He had lived the consequences of that himself, and paid a high price for it. He had never been truly happy again, after he and Marie-Helene split up.

"I don't know how to thank you. I was afraid you were going to warn me to stay away from all of you, and had found out about me somehow."

"I only knew because my father told me. But when I saw you yesterday in church, I knew immediately that you were the one. You looked gorgeous, by the way." He realized that she must have been an incredible model before the explosion. He didn't follow fashion, so didn't recognize her name when their father told him. "I come to Paris once in a while. I'll look you up when I do. And you can call me in New York anytime. Do you know what you're going to do now?"

"I don't." She shook her head. "I keep trying to figure it out. And if he left me anything, I want to do something in his memory, and my mother's, something that helps people, the way they would have wanted to."

"Will you be okay, now that you're not modeling?" He was concerned about her now, as their father had been. She had been through a lot for any human to survive.

"Yes. I had a good time doing it for four years, but I feel like I have to do something better now. Maybe help the victims of other terrorist attacks and Brussels too. There are so many needy wounded people in the world. I was lucky. I survived it, but many of the victims in Paris and Brussels are much worse off than I was." He nodded, and found the thought of it appalling. The savagery of it was breathtaking. He had read some of the reports online after his father told him. He couldn't imagine how Véronique had lived through it. "I'm coming back here again in two and a half months for another surgery. Maybe we could get together then."

"Absolutely. And don't disappear now. We'll have some business matters to take care of soon." He didn't tell her how much money it involved, and she didn't want to know yet. What he had shared with her, and his acceptance, meant far more to her. Her father had given her another gift telling Chip the story, so Chip didn't discover it on his own after his father's death. He had united brother and sister with his blessing, and told Chip what she meant to him.

"I'm easy to find." She smiled at him. "I'm living in my mother's apartment, where I grew up. And I'm here for another ten days, until the doctors release me."

"Dad gave me that number. It's where I called you. And I have the others too, including your cellphone in Paris."

They talked for another hour and he told her stories about their father that helped her know him better and made her laugh and touched her. His sisters sounded a little difficult, and more like their mother, and he didn't deny it, but he said he was close to them in spite of it, and he wanted to protect her from them. He didn't want them to be harsh with her and they might. They were twice her age, and much tougher. Véronique seemed like a gentle person to him, in spite of all she'd been through, and her enormous success as a model. She wasn't full of herself, or bitter, or angry, even about their father, who had ignored her for so long. She was just grateful for the time she had had with him, however brief, and now she was grateful for Chip's friendship and kindness to her.

She left him outside the Carlyle and walked home in the crisp air. She had a lot to think about, and a lot to be grateful for. Now she had a brother. She wasn't entirely alone in the world after all.

Dr. Talbot and Dr. Dennis met with her ten days later, and both were very pleased with what they saw. The scars on her arms and legs and the ones on her stomach were noticeably better, and some had almost disappeared. They weren't nearly as shocking. And the scars on her face had lightened remarkably. They weren't gone by any means, but they didn't appear as deep or as angry, and the smaller one near her jawline had vanished. Phillip Talbot was very pleased with the results. He thought they would get even more improvement with the next surgery. They would never disappear completely, but eventually they would no longer be the first thing one saw about her. He wanted to give her a face she could live with comfortably, without shocking people. He didn't want her to be ashamed, or want to hide. He said the same thing Doug had, that she was a beautiful woman with scars, but she was still spectacularly beautiful. She wasn't The Scars. They were something that life and circumstances had added to her, but they didn't define her. She was beginning to see it differently herself.

They kept gauze on her face just to protect it, and told her she could take it off in a week. In all her injured areas, the skin was thinner now and had to be treated more carefully. They set a date for her next surgery in March, which oddly was on the anniversary of the attack in Brussels, but somehow that seemed fitting to her.

She had dinner with Doug before she left and showed him the improvement, and he was impressed and encouraged for her. She told him about Chip, and called Chip before she left. He told her to take care and he would contact her soon about financial matters.

Then she flew home to Paris, and had to face the same painful phenomenon she'd experienced before, expecting to see her mother when she walked into the apartment, and no one was there, just the echo of her own footsteps resonating in the empty apartment. She wondered how long it would take her to get used to the reality that her mother was gone, and even in their familiar home, she was alone now.

Two days after she got home, she had a phone call that shocked her. A major French television network, the most important one, contacted her. They were preparing a documentary, covering the anniversary of the attack in Brussels, and honoring the surviving victims. They wanted to know if she would be the spokesperson and principal guest to narrate it. They were planning to interview all of the survivors, particularly the injured ones, many of whom, she learned, were still in hospitals, and many had not yet received government benefits, which represented a financial crisis for most of them. She was able to support herself with her savings and what her mother had left her, but many couldn't. She thought it was a noble project, but she told them flatly that there was no way she would participate in it. She preferred to recover quietly in the shadows.

"Do you think that's fair to your fellow victims?" the producer who had called her said somewhat harshly. "You are an enormous presence. You have a name and a face that everyone recognizes. You have a voice you can use to speak up on their behalf, many of them don't, some of them can't even speak now, or barely speak French. We've tracked them all down, we know where they are, so many in hospitals, and you could show what an event like this does to people. You even lost your own mother. When people hear the word 'injured,' it conjures up a visit to the emergency room, and two hours later they go home. Some of these people have had over seventy surgeries. If I tell the story, I'm just another commentator. If *you* tell the story, everyone will listen. It doesn't matter if you cry or choke up, people will want to hear it from you. And on top of it you're a beautiful woman." What he said was powerful and unnerved her. She felt anxious and panicked just listening to him.

"I have very bad scars on my face," she said angrily. "I'm not making public appearances, and I'm still having surgeries myself."

"That's my point. No one knows that. Are you still modeling?"

"No, I can't." She sounded annoyed. She hated how pushy he was.

"Exactly. There are scores of people who can no longer work, nurses, secretaries, teachers, mothers, who have lost their arms and legs and can't take care of their children, a doctor who can no longer practice. Don't let the world think that it's over. It's not over for any of the survivors, or the next victims, because it will happen again." Everyone believed that.

"Why me? Why do I have to be the one to do it?"

"Because you're beautiful, and people would rather look at you than someone else. They'll listen to you, and those scars on your face give you a legitimate voice. You owe it to your fellow survivors to do it, and all the victims, including your mother." She wanted to hang up on him when he said that, but she didn't. What he said was very compelling, but she didn't want it to be true.

"I'm not going to be the poster child for anti-terrorism," she said angrily.

"Why not? What better cause is there? We did a film on the Bataclan and the response was overwhelming." She had wanted to do something to help others and had some social importance, but this was too close to home.

"I'll think about it," she said, but didn't intend to. "When do you want to do it? I'm having surgery in New York on the anniversary," she said smugly, thinking that would get her out of it.

"We want to start taping in a week, we have a lot of victims to see, and it'll take us about six weeks to do it."

"I'll let you know," she said, and was relieved to hang up. She hated how pushy he was, but his words had hit their mark, and had a ring of truth to them. She wondered if he was right. Did she have an obligation to the other survivors? But why her? She wasn't convinced by his arguments, only haunted by them.

He called and left messages for her for the next five days, and she didn't return his calls. She didn't want to think about it, or be pressured into doing the show and exposing herself. She could think of dozens of reasons why she didn't want to do it.

She lay awake thinking about it all one night, remembering the stories she had heard from the nurses about other victims, the countless people who had lost limbs, Cyril and her mother and thirty others who had lost their lives. She got up and walked around the apartment, and wound up in her mother's study and said out loud, "Maman, what would *you* do?" And then she knew, because her mother was a selfless person, and would do what was right for the greater good. She tried to be honest about why she didn't want to do it, and she knew it was because she didn't want the world to see her with a ruined face, to see her as imperfect, when she had been so perfect before. Now she was flawed, but as Doug had said, it wasn't her fault, any more than it was her mother's fault that she was dead. Others had done it, and had died in the process. But others like them had to be brought to justice so it couldn't happen again, and those who had paid so dearly with an arm or a leg or their life deserved to be honored and remembered. The show wasn't about her. It was about them.

She went back to bed and slept peacefully for the next few hours, for the first time in days. In the morning she called the producer and growled into the phone. "I'll do it," she said, and he exclaimed with pleasure and thanked her. "When do we start?" she asked.

"As fast as we can," he answered.

"Call me then," she said, and hung up, before she could change her mind.

Chapter 14

The producers of the show called her two days later with the schedule. They were starting the following week. They were going to interview forty-seven of the injured victims, more than thirty of whom were in hospitals awaiting further surgeries, and they were going to interview nine of the families of the victims who had died. She qualified as both.

She told them that as often as possible she would prefer to be photographed or filmed from the left side of her face, but was willing to have the right side filmed too. Her one concession to vanity was that she hired a makeup artist she had worked with many times. He was a genius, and she asked him if he could at least somewhat improve her ugly scars. Even he couldn't make them disappear, but he could do a lot, and if she was going to be in a documentary that was going to be shown all over Europe and possibly the world, she had a right to look as decent as she could. The truth was still there and would be visible. The makeup artist, Jean-Louis, was happy to

189

help, and he told her he'd work for the first week for free, as his contribution to the project. He normally charged a fortune, several thousand euros a day, and the network producing the show had a low budget for it, so she was grateful.

She had told Doug what she was doing, and had been sure he'd tell her she was crazy to expose herself like that. Instead, he said he was proud of her. A little part of her was proud of herself too. It was going to be the hardest thing she'd ever done, but she was the voice for all the wounded, broken people who had barely survived and the thirty-two who had died, so needlessly.

She went to the studio every day to study the research material on the victims, so she could ask them intelligent questions, and understand them better. She wanted to make a valid contribution. She told herself that when the project was over she was not going to become the spokesperson for the victims of the bombing. She was only going to do this once, and told the producers that too. She had been lucky and had survived. This was her way of giving back.

She was so busy she had no time to think of or do anything else. Gabriella came to Paris from Belgium, and Véronique had a quick lunch with her and no time to do anything else. She had a trial makeup session with Jean-Louis, so he could see what would work best to tone down her scars. He stood looking furious while working on her face and she thought he was angry at her.

"Those bastards. You had the most perfect face I've ever worked on. You still do, but then they go and do this . . . this shit . . . this travesty. It's like putting graffiti on the *Mona Lisa,* or carving it up with a knife. Everyone can still see how beautiful you are," he assured her, "but I hate them for what they did."

"Maybe it was meant to teach me a lesson," she said. "That beauty, as we think of it, doesn't matter. One day I'll get old, and I won't look like this anymore. So it happened early, and I have to find other ways to be beautiful, from inside." He stared at her, shocked at what she said.

"You're some kind of saint," he said.

"No, but you have to find a way to live with it. That's true for the people who lost their limbs too. Some of them are remarkable in how they view it and are adjusting to it. It's the ones who are filled with hate or anger or self-pity who don't survive it, or not well."

"I still think you're a saint." When he made her up for the cameras, you could still see her scars, but they didn't look as raw or as frightening. Her recent surgery had calmed them down too. What was shocking was when the camera shot her from the left and you saw the smooth perfection of her face, and then you saw the right, intersected by two deep scars, butchered by the blast. But when she smiled, you forgot everything else. The producers were thrilled to have her associated with the piece.

Filming the victims was grueling. They cried. They told their stories. They showed their severed limbs, and photographs of themselves before the explosion, and right after. The stories were harrowing and heartbreaking, and the families who had lost loved ones tore your heart out with their grief. It made her think of Cyril and his parents again.

They filmed the victims who had done well too, who were fighting to turn it around, to be more because of it, who were in rehab, in wheelchairs, who had gone back to jobs or had to find new ones that could accommodate their disabilities. They all said that government benefits had been slow, and the red tape was endless. Many were in dire financial straits, and unable to pay their rent or feed their kids, if they could no longer work.

What came through in most cases was how brave they were, how hard they were trying a year later to overcome their injuries, to move on, to be philosophical about it. Very few of them were angry or bitter. They talked about how they didn't want to let what had happened ruin their lives, how they refused to add hate to the mix, and were determined to go on and lead good lives.

Véronique and the entire crew cried every day. It was an emotional six weeks while they worked on the documentary. Véronique refused payment for it and contributed her fees to a victims' fund. The film had to be edited and would air on the anniversary of the attack. They had promised to send her a digital copy since she would be in the hospital in the States having her second surgery then.

She felt good about it, as though she had done something meaningful instead of moving furniture around in her apartment, shopping, or seeing friends, which she still wasn't doing except with Gabriella when she came from Brussels for the day, or with Doug in New York.

Chip had sent her some papers, which she hadn't had time to look at carefully, while she was working on the documentary. She finally sat down and read them one night. Her father had left her two million dollars, which was a drop in the bucket compared to what he had left his other children, but she was stunned by his generosity, and still wanted to do something meaningful with it, something that would honor him and her mother. She had no idea what. Her mother had left her enough to live on. She also had the apartment, and what she'd earned herself, which was invested. She didn't need an extravagant life. She wanted to put some good back in the world to counter all the hate.

She was busy with post-production of the show right up until she left for New York. She had to do all the blood work again, in case something had changed. Both doctors found her in good spirits and thought that all her scars looked better, even her face. She told them about the documentary she'd been working on and they were impressed.

It was hard for her to believe that it had been a year since it happened. So much had changed in her life. She had lost her mother, found her father and lost him, and met her brother. Her father had left her an enormous bequest. She had survived. She was going out in public without a mask. Her modeling career had ended abruptly, and she had worked on the documentary and met many of her fellow victims. There was a silent solidarity between them, like survivors of a war, or a ship sinking, or an act of hatred so enormous that no one could understand it. She'd had victories and defeats and losses. Just being alive was a victory, and learning to live with her scars was an act of courage.

She talked to Dr. Dennis after he examined her scars, and she had told him more about the documentary.

"Have you thought any more about coming to Africa to see the hospital there where I volunteer?" he asked her.

"Not really. I've been so busy with the TV show, I haven't had time to think, but I'd like to come." He had spent the month of February there, and had come back to New York to work in March, and was leaving again from mid-April to mid-June. "You could come in April when I go back," he suggested. "I'd like to be there to show you around. Or you could come in May, whatever works for you." She had nothing to do now that she'd finished working on the TV show. "You're welcome to come whenever you like. Where we are is pretty remote, and we don't get many visitors. Injured children are hard to look at, and some people can't handle it," he said simply. He had already shown her which of her scars he would be working on next. Dr. Talbot had explained to her his part of the procedure, on her face. She was pleased with the results so far, and the makeup for the show had worked well, making her face easier to look at for viewers.

She thought about it that night, and told Dick Dennis the next day that she would go in April, a few days after he arrived there himself. He said the timing worked well for him.

Her surgery was the next day, the anniversary of the attack on Zaventem, and of her mother's death as well, and Cyril's. She hadn't heard from his mother again, and didn't expect to. They had lost their only child, and she didn't sound as though she was doing well when she responded to Véronique's sympathy letter, nor was she warm toward Véronique, as though she had led him to his death. His mother needed someone to blame. Many of the survivors did, or some anyway. For the most part they were compassionate, but some of the parents were very bitter, which Véronique could understand.

* * *

She had a hard night that night, remembering the little she did. Still being conscious and waiting to be rescued, while they thought that she was dead and kept running past her, and not having the strength to call out to them, and the endless surgeries once she was out of the coma. She could still smell the odor of the explosion. Sometimes it filled her nostrils in nightmares. Others had mentioned it too, and the smell of blood and torn flesh all around them. She was wide awake when she had to leave for the hospital, and looked serious when her doctors saw her before the surgery.

"Hard night?" Dick Dennis asked her. He suspected it would be, and she nodded.

"Sometimes it still seems like it was yesterday."

"A year isn't a long time," he said gently. "You've come a long way, Véronique. You're doing really well. I'm sorry we have to put you through another surgery. I hope this will be the last one." She wasn't determined to remove every scar, just the worst ones. Both he and Phillip Talbot wanted to give her the best result they could, but didn't want to go to extremes. The scars on her face were the most important ones to work on, because they affected how she felt about herself, and how she interacted with others. She was still very young and had many years ahead of her. They wanted her to have the best life she could, with as few remnants of the explosion as possible. And she had been reclusive in the past year, which seemed a shame at her age.

"We're going to have a good time in Africa," Dick Dennis said to distract her when they put in the IV. There was some sedation in it, and she would begin to relax and get drowsy soon. She wasn't as frightened as she had been the first time. She knew what to expect now, and she trusted both her surgeons implicitly.

"You're going to Africa with Dick?" Phillip Talbot asked her, and she nodded with a sleepy smile.

"Oh God, bugs and snakes and creepy-crawlies," he said, and they all laughed. "He dragged me there once. I'm a city boy, although it's a noble cause."

"Véronique is gutsier than you are," Dick said, and his colleague laughed.

The attendants rolled her to the operating room a few minutes later, and she was fully unconscious shortly after. Both doctors looked at each other over her sleeping form. They wanted the very best for her, she was a great girl and she deserved it. They didn't see the supermodel as she lay there. They saw the brave young woman she had become in the past year, and they had come to admire and respect so much. She had become a favorite patient for both of them, and they wanted to give her the best future they could, and that she deserved.

She went through the same process as three months before, and she was back in the guest apartment three days later, and was recovering even faster this time.

Four days after the anniversary, she checked her computer and saw that they had sent her the digital video of the show. She couldn't wait to see it, and asked Doug if he wanted to watch it with her. His French was good enough to understand most of it, and she could translate the rest for him.

He came with a pizza, and she downloaded it on her laptop. It was a two-hour show, and neither of them said a word for the entire two hours. She saw him wipe his eyes several times, and she cried, even though she had done the interviews and knew the content. But the interviews were so moving that they made her cry every time. They couldn't even finish their pizza, they just sat listening to the people speaking. Everything they said was so heart wrenching, especially the parents of people who had died, and the victims who had been so badly maimed they were unrecognizable. The film had been beautifully edited, and there were no editorial comments. It was all spoken by the subjects, which made it more powerful. Véronique had been respectful with her questions. She looked beautiful on camera most of the time, and at times her own scars were shocking when the camera caught her from certain angles. She winced when she saw her own images and Doug squeezed her hand.

They were both exhausted when they finished watching it, and looked at each other.

"I don't know how you did those interviews," Doug said in hushed tones and he poured himself a glass of wine. She was still on pain meds so she couldn't drink.

"The crew cried constantly and so did I, but I have to admit, they did a good job with it. Sometimes it was just too much, hearing one tragedy after another, but they mixed them up pretty well."

"The whole thing is a tragedy," he said.

"I don't want to be that," she said, "a sad story that people tell. It was awful, and none of us will ever forget it, but we have to go on. I was luckier than a lot of people, and I'm not starving because I lost my job, but I don't want to be a tragic figure, or have people see me that way, or see myself that way."

"I don't see you as a tragic figure," he said with a twinkle in his eye. "You're as big a pain in the ass as you ever were, even now that you're not a superstar." He was teasing her because she had never been difficult, and he had loved working with her. "You're just a has-been now."

"Yeah, I know. That's why they put me on the show, so people would feel sorry for me," she retorted with spirit. But there was no question, she had lost a lot, they all had, even those who had escaped unscathed had the trauma to live with, which was huge. One woman had said that she had no injuries, but she hadn't been able to leave her house in a year. She was too afraid of it happening again. It took a huge amount of courage to get past it, and move forward. Véronique had fought hard for that and still was.

They talked about her trip to Africa for a while after that.

"How long are you going to stay?" he asked her.

"I don't know. A month, maybe two, if I love it. I have nothing to rush home for. I'm going to fly from here." She couldn't face going home again. It killed her walking into the empty apartment, expecting her mother to be there. She wondered how long that would last. It hadn't gotten better yet. But Chip had told her he felt the same way about his father now when he had to go to the apartment to get something. They were such big people in life, that their absence was sorely felt.

She had spoken to Chip several times since she'd gotten back to New York, and she was planning to see him for lunch when she felt better, and wasn't still woozy from the drugs. She felt fine in the apartment, but she didn't feel up to going out yet. They had talked about the money she had inherited, and he was going to continue to invest it for her. She hadn't told Doug about it. It was just too much money and it was embarrassing to talk to normal people about amounts like that. She was still shocked he had left it to her, but Chip seemed fine about it. He knew her now, and that she wasn't some gold digger, and his father had genuinely loved her mother, who had sacrificed so much for him. He didn't think his sisters would see it that way, and they would never know, the way their father had set it up. He had been an estate and tax attorney before he was in politics, so had done it well.

Doug stayed with Véronique until late that night, sensing that she didn't want to be alone after watching the video. The firsthand accounts brought all the details back to her, some of which she didn't even know until she worked on the film. The doctors and surgeons were always very discreet about the patients, and they had been about her too, which she had appreciated.

"Don't stay in Africa too long," he said wistfully, "I'm going to miss you."

"It sounds really interesting. The little hospital where Dr. Dennis works only treats children, and their injuries sound very severe. Kind of like Brussels," she said thoughtfully. "I wonder if that will ever fade from our minds," she said with a sigh.

"Everything fades eventually, good and bad," he said. "Good fades faster, and bad takes longer." She was trying not to hold on to the terrible memories, but there were so many of them. And with time and distance, the memories were clearer, and the images so hard.

She sat thinking about it all after Doug left. He had been such a good friend to her ever since it happened.

The doctors were happy with the results again. More scars had disappeared on her legs and arms, although she still had many. The one on her stomach was less terrifying, as was the one on her ankle, where she had nearly lost her foot. That battle had been won before she even regained consciousness from the coma. She had pins in her ankle now, but didn't feel them. The scars on her face had gotten much softer, the sharp edges had been smoothed down, the scarlet color had faded, and the area around them was normal skin tone now. There were still two deep grooves, but they didn't look as angry, or as though they had been inflicted with an axe. Everything was getting gentler with time. The doctors had warned her to stay out of the sun in Africa and wear a hat at all times, but Dick Dennis would be there if she had a problem, and she could always come home if it was serious, or back to New York to see Dr. Talbot.

She saw Chip for lunch two days before she left, as promised.

"You look terrific," he complimented her, and she didn't know if he meant her scars or her general appearance. She was wearing a pink sweater and coat with jeans. She'd had to buy clothes to wear in Africa because she didn't have the right things with her, or even own some of them. She was leaving some things at Doug's apartment that she couldn't use in Angola. "You look more relaxed," Chip said to her.

"At least the surgery is behind me. This should be the last one, unless any of the shrapnel moves around, but I'm hoping it won't." She knew it could create some life-threatening situations if it did, and block an artery or a vital organ, even her heart. But what was left hadn't moved in a year, and hopefully never would. They were going to leave the pins in her ankle. There was no reason to take them out.

They talked about how his congressional campaign was going, his kids, and his divorce. He liked talking to her, even though she was young. She had seen a lot of life, more than most people, between her modeling career and surviving a terrorist attack and a year of surgery. She was wise beyond her years, more than his own kids who were nearly the same age. She could tell he was upset about his divorce. His wife had gotten greedy, and they were battling over their house, and his inheritance.

"Be careful in Angola," he warned her, "and let me know how you are. I just found you, I don't want to lose you." He looked serious as he said it.

"You won't." She smiled at him. She was made of strong stuff and he knew it. His father had admired her for it too.

She left for the airport with a single suitcase, packed tightly with all the things Dick Dennis said she needed. Shorts, long jeans, heavy hiking boots despite the heat, every possible kind of insect repellent, sunscreen to protect her scars, and zinc oxide, pain medication if she needed it, antibiotics in case she got sick, long-sleeved shirts and a few T-shirts, a couple of simple peasant skirts. She didn't bring anything fancy since she'd have no use for it. This was a rough and ready work trip in a small, primitive village on rough terrain. He said that even the nuns wore hiking boots with their habits. He had left a few days earlier, and would have time to settle in before she got there.

He had arranged for a room for her in the convent. The nurses lived there too. It all sounded like a great adventure. She rode to the airport in a cab, her passport in a small zippered pouch on her belt. She had enough money with her for emergencies, and for once she didn't even think about her scars or how anyone would react to them. As far as she knew, she had recovered from Zaventem. She felt free and could hardly wait to discover Angola. The nightmare of the past year was finally behind her. She was a free woman, heading for her future, and all the surprises it had in store for her. She intended to reach out and grab them. She wasn't the same woman she'd been a year before, and she could sense that she wouldn't be the same after this trip either. Everything was new to her, and every day was a gift.

Chapter 15

Véronique flew to Luanda, the capital of Angola, on Emirates airlines with a stop in Dubai. The flight was long, and in Luanda, she took a short flight to Cuito Cuanavale. There were two flights a week from Luanda to Cuito Cuanavale, and the hospital was in a rural area nearly two hours away by car. The HALO Trust was still working on clearing mines for the area, and had made progress, but the surrounding area was not mine-free yet, with devastating effect on the local population, and some horrifying injuries as a result.

She was met at the airport by a young man with a wide ivory smile, whose name was Joachim. He spoke surprisingly good English, with a Portuguese accent. He walked with a limp, but was bright and friendly, and told her as they left the airport, "Dr. Dick saved my legs. I was twelve when my brother and I stepped on a mine. My brother was nine. He was killed. Dr. Dick saved my life," he said proudly, as they drove through the countryside past Cuito Cuanavale. There were goats along the side of the road and chickens, children playing in the dirt, women in colorful clothes, panos, which were wraparound batik garments, some with bright colored cloths around their heads or balancing baskets. Joachim was driving a battered old red Ford truck and wearing a colorful shirt and jeans. He had brought some bottled water for her. She had been traveling for twenty-seven hours by then. She was hot and dusty when they arrived at a small compound, with a tiny church, a large wooden building built by the locals with a sign outside that read "Saint Matthew's Hospital," and another large building that looked like a school. There was a group of nuns walking up the front steps in immaculate white nursing habits in contrast to all the bright colors around them. There were masses of bougainvillea and other flowers she didn't recognize, and the nuns were laughing, as they turned to see who the new arrival was, just as Dr. Dennis walked out of the hospital. He had been watching for her from the office he used on the main floor. There were clusters of locals sitting on the ground, with small children and old people who were there to support the children they had brought to the hospital for treatment. Some of them were cooking.

"Welcome!" Dick Dennis called out to her, and hurried toward her. He was wearing a short white doctor's coat over a Hawaiian shirt, with jeans and hiking boots, and he hugged Véronique as soon as he reached her. She had traveled in jeans and hiking boots too. The nuns came back down the steps of the building that looked like a school and were smiling as they came toward her. One was tall, heavyset, and older. Another looked barely older than Véronique and had an angelic face, and the other two were somewhere in their thirties, as closely as one could tell with the short white coifs of their habits. Their habits just reached their ankles, and they were wearing hiking boots too.

"Sister Anne," Dick Dennis said, introducing the older one, who beamed at Véronique. Sister Claire was the younger one, and the two in the middle were Sister Rita and Sister Charity. He had decided not to explain the circumstances of Véronique's stay before she came, and to let her do it, if she chose to. He didn't want to precede her with a tragic story if she didn't want to share it. All four nuns looked delighted to see her.

"There are twelve of us here," Sister Anne explained, referring to the nuns, "you can figure out the names later. We have a room all ready for you." She pointed to the building they had just come from. "That's our monastery, our dormitory, as we call it. The nurses live with us too, and we have some guest rooms for visitors. We're so happy you've come to visit." Véronique could hear that Sister Rita was French when she spoke to her. They were the happiest looking women she'd ever met.

"I'll give you a tour of the hospital after you settle in," Dick Dennis promised. "You must be exhausted." But she didn't look it. She looked fresh and excited to be there.

"I slept on the plane," she explained. Sister Claire took her bag from her, and they led her to the convent. There were people milling around in the common area between all the buildings. There were trees for shade and flowers everywhere. It looked like paradise to

Véronique, and she was thrilled to be there. She felt like she was walking into a girls' school. There were more nuns in the halls, and a few nurses in white uniforms.

"We're one big happy family," Sister Claire explained. "There are ten nurses as well as the twelve nuns. Most of the nurses are British. Sister Rita is French, like you. And there are two Australians, and an American. We do a lot of surgeries when the visiting doctors are here. They rotate in and out for a month or two at a time. Dr. Dennis is here three months of the year. It all rolls pretty smoothly. Are you a nurse?" the young nun asked Véronique.

"No, I'm just interested in what you do here. Dr. Dennis told me about it, and invited me to come and see, so here I am," she said, feeling like the new girl at school.

"We gave you a single room," Sister Charity volunteered. "Most of the nurses share but they're on different shifts so it works pretty well. We just finished our shift, so we come back to the monastery for our evening prayers before dinner."

"How many children do you have in the hospital?" Véronique asked, as they walked to her room.

"Usually around eighty. We can handle close to a hundred in an emergency. They bring us children from the surrounding areas and villages. Some of the minefields haven't been fully explored and cleaned up yet. And sometimes we get children who have lived with their injuries for a long time and were never properly treated."

"That's a lot of children." Véronique looked impressed.

"A lot of children need us here," Sister Anne said. "A lot of injuries, and serious accidents, severed limbs, infections that go untreated, and then require amputations. We keep our doctors busy."

They had reached her room by then. Sister Anne opened the door, and Véronique was surprised to see a big airy room with a fan turning overhead on the ceiling. There was mosquito netting over the bed, which they called "bed nets," and all the furniture was painted white. There were screens on the windows, and gauzy curtains. She had expected a small dark cell, and instead everything was clean and bright, including the bed, which was freshly made for her and looked very inviting after her long trip, but she was determined to stay awake until bedtime, to get on their regular time.

"There's a shower down the hall," Sister Charity explained. "Just put your name down on the schedule. You have priority since you're a guest." Sister Claire giggled. "The dining room and the kitchen are at the far end of the building. Breakfast is from six to seven, when the shift changes, lunch is from twelve to one, and dinner is at six. We have local women who do the cooking, and the food is delicious, mostly local dishes. There's a cottage where the resident doctor lives, behind the hospital. Do you need anything?" she asked with wide eyes and a warm smile.

"No, this all looks wonderful." She smiled at them. They were a perfect welcoming committee.

"Are you hungry? Would you like something to eat?" one of the sisters asked her.

"No, I'm fine." She was too tired to be hungry, and too excited to want to waste time on a meal.

She washed her face and hands in the sink in the room after they left, brushed her hair, and went to find Dr. Dennis in the hospital. He was waiting for her in his office, and she could see his cottage from the window.

"It's simple but it all functions very efficiently. We get donations from organizations all around the world," he told her. "The nuns and the nurses are wonderful. Is your room all right?"

"It's perfect." She smiled at him. "Thank you for inviting me. I didn't know what to expect."

"I'll drive you out to the villages tomorrow and show you around. Would you like a tour of the hospital now?"

"I'd love it." He looked so proud of the facility, and he seemed more at ease here than he did in his fancy New York office. There was an amazing contrast between the two. It was hard to believe he was comfortable in both, and practiced in two such different environments.

"I live to come out here," he said to her. "It's a whole different world, and gives meaning to my life. You can really make a difference here, more so than for most of our patients in New York. When I first came here, the civil war was still on, and the casualties were brutal. That's how the minefields started." He took her through the wards then. There were sixteen children in each ward, and two nuns and two nurses to care for them. The wards were designated according to how ill the children were. There was a surgical ward for children who had recently had surgery, with fewer children in it. Their families hovered around their beds, or sat on the floor, or sat on their beds and held them.

"Their families are very much a part of their care. Some come from very far away, others are from nearby villages." You could see that it was a culture of family as they huddled together.

She observed as she walked through the wards with him that many of the children were missing limbs, and only had stumps.

More than half of the land-mine injuries in Angola were children. They collected sticks for firewood in the fields, and the mines exploded. The children all got excited when they saw Dr. Dick, and he stopped to hug several of them and talk to them and their parents in Portuguese or Umbundu. He spoke both, and two other native dialects. It was a whole different experience for Véronique after the military hospital in Belgium, and her recent surgeries in New York. This had a whole other flavor, which combined local traditions and culture with Western medicine.

"I bring in a lot of American medicines they can't get here. It's a big help, and we get shipments from Germany and France too, and the United Kingdom. We're grateful for whatever we can get. We run it on a tight budget. We don't have a lot of funds, but we make it stretch. Most of the families do their own cooking on the grounds. Although we're primarily surgical, we give all of them vaccinations they'd never get otherwise." She could see how much he loved it, and how he thrived on the work he did there, and how much he cared about his patients. All the children waved and called him by name as he walked her through the immaculate hospital.

They went back to his office after the tour, and she had noticed how neat and precise the place was, and the equipment looked surprisingly new and up to date.

"We have a rotation of doctors from the United States, France, and the UK. I stay here longer than the others. Most of them can't take that much time off from their practices. But Phillip is very good about it. He knows how much I love it here, and letting me do this was one of my conditions of opening the practice with him. If he needs me, and gets too swamped, I can always fly back the way I did in March, but I like to be here as much as possible. I'll be here now till mid-June. Do you know how long you're staying?"

"I haven't figured that out yet. I'd like to be useful while I'm here, as a volunteer in the hospital. It's the only service I can provide."

"We can use all the help we can get," he said warmly. "The nurses and the nuns will let you know how you can help. Sometimes they just need you to sit with a child who's come out of surgery, if we're shorthanded. Some of the children get injured by dangerous farm equipment. We have a full house most of the time. The nuns used to run the place themselves with a doctor who came through once a month. We've recruited a lot of volunteer medical staff since then. There's always a doctor on duty here now. We had some Australian docs here last year who were terrific." The feeling was very international, while respecting the African traditions and how they cared for their sick. The nurses spent a lot of time teaching parents to change dressings, to avoid infection.

By the time she left his office, it was almost six o'clock. He had more patients to see and post-op patients to check. Véronique wandered back to the dormitory, and went to find the dining room, and when she did, it was a big room with long refectory tables, and more fans circulating overhead. The smells from the kitchen were delicious. The nurses she had already met in the wards walked in as she was looking around, and invited her to sit at their table.

More nurses joined them a few minutes later, and within half an hour all the tables were full with laughing, talking, chatting women. It looked and sounded like a girls' school for adults, only no one was glum or unhappy to be there. There was an atmosphere of real joy and pride about what they were doing, and it was contagious. Several of the nuns made a point of introducing Véronique to the other nuns and nurses. They were all interested in where she was from, and how she had heard about them, and asked how long she was staying. They were an open, friendly group of women, who all made her feel welcome. They had chicken with delicate spices to eat for dinner, cornmeal, plantain, and some vegetables she didn't recognize but it all tasted delicious. After she had eaten, the trip caught up with her. She could hardly keep her eyes open, as she headed to her room. She brushed her teeth, put on pajamas, and crawled under the mosquito netting, and before she could put her head on the pillow, after she turned out the light, she was instantly asleep. So far, she loved everything she'd seen and everyone she'd met at Saint Matthew's. It felt like coming home.

The next morning, after breakfast at six, she took a quick shower according to the schedule, and arrived at the hospital as Dr. Dennis was starting his rounds. He had two nurses with him, whom she hadn't met yet, and he introduced her. Both were British, Prudence and Felicity. She accompanied them to the wards, and observed what they were doing. Many of the children were severely damaged after accidents, and several of them had disfigured faces, mostly due to the minefields. One little girl, who appeared to be about four or five, cried when he checked her dressing. She had been in a mine explosion when walking to the river with her mother. She had deep scars on her face that looked similar to Véronique's. She smiled at the little girl, and pointed to her own face. The little girl stared at her and stopped crying, and asked her mother in their dialect how the lady had hurt her face. Felicity translated it for Véronique, and Véronique answered without feeling self-conscious, possibly for the first time.

"A big explosion," she said to the mother, gesticulating with her arms to show how big it was, and said "Boom!" loudly to go with it. The little girl laughed when she did, and let Dr. Dennis examine her. She watched Véronique with interest the entire time.

The little girl smiled again when they left her, looked at Véronique and said "Boom!" herself and pointed to Véronique, and they all laughed.

"Yes, boom!" Véronique said again, and pointed to her face. Then the child said something to her mother, which Felicity translated again.

"She says you are very pretty," Felicity said with a smile.

"Thank you!" Véronique answered her. "You are very pretty too," she said, pointing to the little girl and smiling, as Felicity translated again. The little girl giggled and hid her face in her pillow. They moved on and Véronique was still smiling. The nurses didn't comment on the exchange or ask further details about the scars on Véronique's face. "Boom" seemed to cover it.

When they finished the doctor's rounds, he took Véronique out to the car he drove while he was there. All the doctors used it. "I thought I'd give you a look at the nearby villages." He spoke the local dialects well enough to converse with the patients easily and occasionally used a translator for difficult cases, so he got all the information he needed accurately. He was deeply committed to the people in the area and the goals of the HALO Trust, to make Angola mine-free in the future. Their name stood for "Hazardous Area Life-support Organization" and he'd known many of the young people in the villages since they were born.

They followed a deeply rutted road and stopped at a village about ten miles away with a lot of mud huts and a few shaky-looking small wooden buildings. Several of the residents recognized him and greeted him warmly, as they walked around. A stream ran alongside the town, where women were washing clothes and carrying vessels of water and baskets on their heads. Most of them wore sandals, many were barefoot. Their poverty was evident, but they were friendly and welcoming to Dick and Véronique. No one looked unfriendly or unhappy. A few were eating, and there were cows nearby.

"The cows belong to the chief," he said to her, "to show that he's the richest man in the village." As they got in the car to leave, a man ran up to them and tried to hand a young goat to Dick. He kept bowing and thanking the doctor in Kikongo, and Dick pointed to the car to show he couldn't take the goat with him, and the donor accepted it back in good humor.

"We give them free services," he explained to her, "but that's not how they like to do things, so they bring us melons, and chickens, an occasional goat or a young pig. They like to pay their debts. They're honorable people. I always tell Phillip about it, and wonder what would happen if our patients gave us pigs or goats in exchange for Botox shots. That could be interesting." She laughed, thinking of how luxurious their office was. A pig running around the office would definitely be entertaining.

They visited several other villages that were similar, Chiumbo and Lioema, and then looped back to the hospital on another rutted old road. She had seen numerous injured children during their drive. There were many of them, and she could see why their hospital treated so many patients on an ongoing basis.

"The roads get washed out sometimes during the rainy season. It's harder to get to them then, and for them to come to us. We have an old truck with four-wheel drive, but it's not reliable. We need so many things here. We have to prioritize very carefully. The medical equipment and supplies come first." She could see a need for many kinds of equipment. He said the hospital existed on donations of the material they needed and medical supplies. But whatever they got was never enough. And their available funds were limited.

It was after lunchtime by the time they got back to the hospital, and she went to get something to eat in the kitchen, and then to clean up after the drive over the rough roads. She took off her hiking boots and jeans, which were all dusty. Prudence, one of the English nurses, dropped by to say hello while she was changing, and saw the scars on her legs.

"Was that boom too?" They both smiled, thinking of the little girl with the scars on her face in the ward that morning. Véronique nodded and put on fresh jeans.

"Yes, it was. It was a big boom."

"Military?" she asked her. She had been an army nurse for five years, before she left the military and came to Africa to Saint Matthew's, recruited by a doctor she knew who volunteered there.

"Brussels airport a year ago," Véronique said simply.

"Shit," Prudence said, making a face. "The world is a crazy place these days. I used to see injuries like that when I was an army nurse and something went wrong on maneuvers." She had recognized the shrapnel wounds.

"I'm okay now," Véronique said, and meant it.

"What did you do before that, and before you came to Africa?" she asked, curious about her. She looked familiar.

"I was a model before the boom," she said with a smile, and Prudence stared at her.

"Oh my God, Véronique Vincent? I saw every magazine you were ever in. You were my idol. I dyed my hair the color of yours once. It looked terrible on me. That really is rotten luck. I wondered why I hadn't seen you in a year. I thought maybe you had a baby and took a year off."

"No, I took a year off after the boom, in a military hospital in Brussels. I'm trying to figure out the rest now."

"Will you go back to modeling?" She looked anxious for her.

"Not with this." She pointed to her face. "It looks better than it did, but it won't go away. So here I am. It sounds crazy, but I like it here," she said, smiling at Prudence.

"It is crazy, but we all do. That's why we stay. They need the help so badly. You go to bed at night knowing you've made a difference. I didn't feel that way in the army, or in a hospital in London afterward. Our doctors at Saint Matthew's do a great job. It makes you proud to work here, although we don't have much to work with. We wing it a lot."

"I can see why you love it," Véronique said, as they walked toward the dining room together.

"I hope you stay for a while. We can always use a spare pair of hands."

"That's why I'm here." They walked back to the hospital together, and Véronique went to volunteer her services to the nurses in the wards. They put her to work bringing trays of bandages while they changed dressings. She was all too familiar with what they used. She had seen it all in Belgium.

After that, she helped make beds, and colored with crayons with two little girls. Her little friend from the morning waved at her across the ward and shouted "Boom!" and then laughed uproariously, and Véronique laughed too.

By the end of the day, she didn't know how she would have described what she'd done all day, mostly menial tasks, making things easier for the nuns and nurses, but the day went by, and many days like it. She rapidly settled into a routine of making herself available to all of them. She was the only non-medical volunteer around for the moment, and everyone was grateful for her help, her willingness, and her good humor. She was happy there. She felt as though she had found a niche and she belonged. Dr. Dennis observed her and crossed her in the halls frequently. She looked happy and at ease. The discomforts and primitive conditions didn't bother her, and she got along with everyone. She had made friends among the nuns and nurses. The children loved her. She had never thought she was good with children, nor was particularly interested in them. But here it was different. She liked being around them, and helping wherever she could. She felt comfortable in her own skin for the first time in a year. She was in the right place at the right time. Even six months before would have been too soon. She wasn't ready then, but she was now. She felt competent, useful, and connected.

She'd been there for a month when she asked Dick Dennis if anyone had ever made a film here, showing what they did and the children they cared for. It could help them raise money. He thought about it for a minute. There was film of Princess Diana when she came out there, but that was a long time ago.

"No one here has ever had the expertise to do that, the time, the interest, the funds, or the connections."

"Would that be helpful to you?" Véronique asked him.

"Of course. It's hard describing what it's like here. It's so foreign to people back home, they really don't understand and can't visualize it." She reminded him about the French TV documentary she'd been part of, about the victims and survivors of Zaventem.

"It was on French television, but you could send copies of a show like that to fundraise elsewhere, if they were to do something like it here. Do you want me to call the producer?"

"I'd love it. We can use all the publicity we can get, to raise interest, in Europe or the States."

"I'll call the producer," she promised, and did the next day. Olivier Berger, the producer of the Zaventem show, was intrigued by her suggestion to come and do a documentary in Angola to show the hospital and the patients and the villages they served, and the eclectic international medical staff, some of whom were even French. And the issue of still active land mines was an important one.

"I'm committed for the rest of the month," he said, "but if I get the go-ahead, we could come out with a crew in early June. Would that work for you?"

"I'd have to ask. I'm just a visitor here, a volunteer. I know the doctor who's running it right now. He's here for three months a year. He's American. But they rotate British and French doctors too."

"I'll check it out here with my bosses and get back to you. They might like it. We're trying to do more of these real-life documentaries, and they can't all be tragedies. This might be a very interesting story." And the children made it upbeat and very poignant.

"I think you'd be impressed," she told him, and told Dick Dennis about the call and he thanked her.

Olivier called her back a week later. "They love it. They gave me permission to go ahead and do it with a small crew. How do I set it up?" She had him call Dick Dennis, and they organized everything. The French crew was coming on the first of June, and Dick would still be there then. Véronique was pleased that it had worked. They were going to put Saint Matthew's Hospital on the map. They needed help so desperately, and it was a wonderful feeling doing whatever she could, for all the right reasons.

Chapter 16

A week after Véronique had spoken to Olivier Berger about a documentary about Saint Matthew's, a British journalist, Patrick Weston, showed up on his own. He was a friend of one of the other doctors on the rotation, a British doctor, and he had come to write an article about the work they were doing there. He spoke to Dick Dennis, who liked him, and was impressed by his credentials. He had written for some very prestigious publications. After talking to him, Dick gave him carte blanche to look around. He was going to take some photographs to go with the story. He was a freelancer, and planned to sell the piece when he got back to London.

He was young and personable and seemed very serious. He had gone to Oxford, and was thirty-four years old. He had tousled sandy blond hair and blue eyes and looked very British.

He interviewed several of the nuns, and most of the nurses, as well as Dick. They gave him one of the guest rooms in the dormitory. He was very unobtrusive, and got some wonderful shots of the nuns laughing, the nurses working, the children in the wards and their families, and he talked to Dick Dennis at length about the medical side of the story. It was several days before he got around to Véronique. She had already heard that he had gone to Oxford. His credentials were excellent, and he'd published some articles in the States as well.

Véronique was sitting in the shade for a few minutes, after a morning spent in the ward, and he came to sit down next to her. He smiled when he sat down, and glanced at her.

"I keep wanting to catch a word with you, but you never seem to stop. You're busy every time I look, holding a child, or consoling a mother, or making a bed. Are you a nurse?" Unlike the others, she didn't wear a uniform.

"No, I'm just here as a friend."

"You're French?" He heard her accent, and had assumed she was American or British, like most of the others. She nodded.

"My father was American," she added proudly.

"What brought you here?" There was something about her that intrigued him, and he hadn't figured out what. She kept her distance, although she was friendly, but guarded.

"Dr. Dennis. I met him in New York, and he told me about it. It sounded interesting, so I came to see for myself." In the meantime, she had gotten passionate about a mine-free world too.

"Just like that?" She nodded with a mysterious smile. He had noticed the scars but didn't ask her about it. He was very polite.

"Yes, just like that," she confirmed.

"Are you a medical person of some kind, if not a nurse?" He couldn't peg her.

"No, I liked the sound of what they're doing for these children. They do wonderful work. I've been here for more than a month, and I'm amazed every day. I've gotten interested in projects that people dedicate themselves to, to make a serious difference in the world."

"That's noble of you." He smiled at her. There was something about her face that seemed familiar. "Why do I get the feeling that I've seen you somewhere?"

"I must look like someone you know," she said coolly.

"Not that I can think of. I don't meet women who look like you every day, Véronique," he said, and she looked embarrassed.

"A wanted poster in the post office perhaps?" she teased him.

He laughed. "Why? Have you been in prison?"

"Not lately." He smiled at her answer. She was playing with him, and he suspected there was something behind it. He had a good nose for people, and she wasn't giving him answers.

"Are you here incognito?" he teased her back.

"Not at all."

"Well, you're definitely a hard worker," he complimented her.

"I love being here. I'd only been to Johannesburg before."

"For work?"

She nodded. She noticed that there was something sad about his eyes, as though something bad had happened to him. It was a look she understood and it aroused her interest about him.

"It's healing being here," he said, and she nodded, and stood up. She agreed with him but felt she'd said enough.

"It's time for lunch," she said, and he stood up too. He watched her move ahead of him up the steps of the dormitory, and it was driving him crazy. He knew he had seen her somewhere before.

He sat down next to Prudence in the dining hall, and Véronique sat down with the nuns. Prudence was flirting mildly with Patrick. She had a boyfriend in London, but she hadn't seen him in months. They were going to meet in Zimbabwe in August. She noticed Patrick staring at Véronique as she chatted with the nuns, and he said something to Prudence about it.

"I don't know why, but I have the feeling I've seen her somewhere before." Prudence didn't answer for a minute and nodded.

"You and the entire world," she said in a low voice, and then said even more softly, "does the name Véronique Vincent ring any bells?" He looked startled, and stared at her.

"The model?" He glanced back at Véronique then, and there it was. It clicked. "Oh good lord." He could see the right side of her face as he stared at her from the distance, and the scars in all their glory. "What happened? A car accident ended it?" He thought she must have gone through a windshield to have scars like that.

Prudence was serious when she answered. "Something a lot worse."

"What could be worse than that?"

"You'll have to ask her about it. It's not my secret to tell."

So he hadn't been wrong when he guessed that she was there incognito. There was something mysterious about her, as though she was hiding something. He went to his room after lunch, and googled her. He got a million of her modeling pictures one after the other, looking more spectacular in each one. Then the recent documentary on French television came up. He clicked the link and watched the beginning of it. He spoke enough French to understand it all. Then he knew the story. She obviously didn't want to talk about it, or she would have told him. But she wasn't hiding it either, if she had been the main interviewer on the TV show. He got the feeling that she'd be upset if he asked. His heart ached as he listened to the stories, and then he came to the part where she explained her part in it and what had happened. He felt as though he had opened a Pandora's box and he shouldn't have. But it explained why she was here in a remote part of Africa, obviously looking for some new meaning to life after what had happened. He felt overwhelmed with sorrow for her, living with the scars she had, and losing a major career couldn't have been easy for her. A career that had obviously defined her since it was all about her looks. She had said on the show that she had lost her mother in the blast, and a friend who was with them.

He didn't approach her again until late that afternoon, when he found her sitting on the steps of the dormitory before dinner, wearing a big straw hat to shield her from the late afternoon sun. Her wearing it made it look glamorous.

"I like your hat," he said and meant it.

"Thank you." She smiled up at him. He didn't know how to broach the subject and tell her he knew who she was. It sounded offensive, as though he was prying, and he didn't want to upset her.

"Would you let me take a photograph of you for my article?" He'd taken pictures of everyone else, so it wasn't an odd request.

"No," she said simply and firmly.

"Why not?" he said boldly.

"Why do you think? I don't like having my photograph taken." She thought it should have been obvious to him.

"The left side of your face is perfect. I could take you in profile, with the Angolan landscape behind you."

"That would be cheating," she said, frowning at him.

"No, it wouldn't."

"Yes, it would. That's not how I look anymore."

"The scars don't make a difference. You're still incredibly beautiful," he said solemnly, impressed by her honesty and her courage.

"Thank you for saying so, but I don't think so."

"Then you're wrong. The scars aren't you or all that's left of you. They were added to you. They didn't replace you. They don't cancel out how beautiful you are."

"Thank you." She decided to be honest with him, to some extent. She looked him in the eye, and it struck her again how sad his eyes were. "I don't want to be an object of pity, or look like a freak."

"There's nothing pitiful about you. You're here. You're in Angola, you're helping people, making a huge difference, as you put it. You're not sitting home and crying or brooding, that's admirable, not pitiful. I'd say you have the upper hand. You're a strong woman. If you weren't, you wouldn't be here. This isn't exactly the Ritz in Paris." She laughed.

"You don't know how I got the scars." He could tell that she didn't like to talk about it.

"No, I don't," he said, not liking the fact that he did and was lying to her. He liked her, and he didn't want to lie to her. "No, that's not true," he corrected himself and she was surprised. "I googled you when I figured out who you are." He didn't want to rat out Prudence and say that she had told. "So I do know. You're alive, Véronique, alive enough to be here and doing good work. The bad guys didn't win. You did. And I'll tell you something that I don't usually tell people either. I was in Paris at the Bataclan, a year ago last November. My wife wanted to go to the concert. I hate that kind of music, and I went for her because it was in Paris. She was shot and died in my arms. We'd been married for six months. She was a fantastic woman, everything I ever dreamed of. And I would give anything to have her back, with a thousand scars, or no arms and legs, instead of having lost her. These attacks are savage. They don't just kill people, they kill people inside even if they survive, like you and me. Don't let them do that to you. Don't let them win. They killed her and they destroyed my life. Fuck the scars, Véronique. You're incredibly beautiful, even *with* the scars. You're doing the right thing being here. You don't need to hide that side of your face, or even owe people an explanation for it, and surely not an apology. You are still beautiful, and you will be until your teeth fall out and you go bald." She laughed and so did he.

"Why should I go bald? Isn't this enough?" She looked incensed, or pretended to be.

"Well, eventually you'll be toothless and bald like the rest of us. Until then, you are still the most gorgeous woman on the planet, scars and all. And you are certainly not pitiful."

She stared at him for a moment, stood up, and put her hands on her hips. "Fine, go ahead, take my picture."

He couldn't believe she'd said it. She was ordering him to. "Like that, with you scowling at me? You look like you're going to kick me. I will *not* take your picture."

"You called me bald and toothless!" She appeared to be outraged and he laughed at her.

"I did not. I said you *will* be bald and toothless, I did *not* say you already are."

"Well, I'm not, so take my picture," and then her voice softened and she grew serious, "and I'm sorry about your wife," she said gently.

"So am I. She was fantastic. Not as beautiful as you, but no one is. She was a great woman and I loved her. She was full of courage, like you." She sensed it was true. "She was half Italian and half English, fire and ice. She was an incredibly talented journalist, far better than I am. I write junk compared to her. She wanted to write a novel, and she would have written a great one. We came from two different worlds. I came from a stuffy, pompous family of upper class intellectual snobs. Her father owned a trattoria in Venice. She had none of the prejudices I grew up with, and she turned me into a human being. And then, she was gone and nothing made sense anymore. Why did I survive and she didn't? She was so much better than I am." He sounded as though he meant it.

"I ask myself that question every day about my mother and the friend I was with. Do you have kids?" she asked him, and he looked like he was going to cry.

"No. She was pregnant. We'd just found out. It's hard to understand the meaning of life after something like that. Why it happened. Why you were there. Why they killed her and not me. They didn't even shoot me. They killed her and I walked out without a scratch. I've been trying to make my peace with that for eighteen months, and I can't."

"You never will. I haven't been able to make sense of it either. Why my mother and my friend died and I didn't. Blind luck maybe. Destiny. You just have to keep going. That's why I'm here. Now are you going to take my picture or not? I used to get a lot of money for having my picture taken, and I'm doing it for free for you. So don't waste it." As she said it, he grinned and picked up his camera, and took a photo of her head-on, scolding him, with both sides of her face showing, the old and the new, the smooth and the scarred with the big floppy hat. She was surprised when he took it. "That's a terrible picture!" she complained.

"No, it's not. It's a great one. And it wasn't cheating. I got both sides of your face, the old and the new, your funny hat, and you were giving me hell. Don't worry. I won't use it. That one's for me. I'm going to frame it. It's perfect. Can I say in the article that you were working here as a volunteer? I won't if you don't want me to." She thought about it for a minute and then nodded.

"I guess there's no harm in that, as long as you don't run that picture." She smiled at him, and they headed up the stairs, toward dinner. "You're complicated," she said to him.

"So are you," he said, and she laughed.

"I guess we have a right to be," she said more gently.

"I think we do." He sat next to her at dinner, and they had an intelligent conversation about a variety of subjects and a nice time together. It seemed odd meeting here, but it felt as though it was meant to be, given their experiences.

"You know, I've never been that open with anyone before about it," he said about what he'd told her. She was easy to talk to, and listened well. He could tell she was a compassionate person.

"Neither have I. I suppose we have that in common." They both knew what it was like, to go to hell and back, and try to make sense of your life afterward. They were both still working on it. She had survivor guilt too, about Cyril and her mother. It was obvious that he was riddled with it, over his wife.

"How long are you going to stay here?" he asked her.

"I don't know. Until I want to go back to Paris. Maybe until I feel good about my life again. I have nothing to go back for. And I want to do some good and put some love back in the world instead of all that hate. You've been there. You know."

"Yes, I do. I suppose we survived for a reason, I just don't know what that is yet," he said.

"Neither do I," she admitted. "I feel like I'm supposed to do something important now. I just don't know what it is. That's why I came here. I wanted to see what they were doing at Saint Matthew's. It's very impressive. And I'm happy here," she said simply.

"I think they're doing very good work. I think you're pretty impressive too, Ms. Vincent," he said, smiling at her.

"And I think you're a terrible photographer. I hope you're a better writer," she said tartly and he laughed.

"I'll send you the article, and you can decide for yourself." He was smiling, and didn't look so sad.

"Thank you." She smiled at him. "They're going to shoot a documentary here in a couple of weeks, for French TV."

"That'll be good for the people here. It'll validate them for fundraising," he confirmed.

"I thought so too. I'd like to help them. They all work so hard." He nodded. He was going to write a glowing article about Saint

Matthew's for just that reason. It was a labor of love, and helped so many people, even those who worked here.

He walked her to her room after dinner, and they had breakfast together the next morning, when they arrived in the dining room at the same time. They chatted a few other times, and two days later he left. He had other places to go in Africa, and other articles to write on spec. She said goodbye to him, and wished him luck. They both had a hard road ahead of them, to recover from what they'd been through. She was feeling better but she could tell that he was still struggling. She had seen it in his eyes. He promised again to send her the article when it came out. And then he left, and drove away. He was flying out in a day or two.

She spent the next two weeks helping Dick to get everything ready for the French TV production group. She thought of Patrick Weston a few times, and assumed she'd never see him again. They were fellow survivors passing in the night. There had been a connection, but opportunity and geography were against them. She didn't give it more thought than that. He was an interesting person, and seemed like a nice man. And she hoped he would recover one day from all he'd lost. It was the best they could do now, with the hands fate had dealt them.

Chapter 17

When Olivier Berger and the French television production company arrived, it turned Saint Matthew's upside down for a while. They followed all of them everywhere with their cameras, into the wards, the operating room, into the convent, and to the nearby villages. They interviewed all of them about what they were doing there, why they had come, why they stayed. They wanted the viewers to know everything about the people working there and what they were doing for the children of Angola, with the limited material and resources they had on hand, and the challenges they were facing, with active mines still in the ground.

They interviewed Dick Dennis extensively, and Véronique briefly, since she played the smallest role there and she was newly arrived. She said how much it meant to her to be there, and how it had changed her life, after the attack in Brussels. She said it was the first thing that had given new meaning to her life.

And knowing what they had done before, Véronique was sure

that they would make a beautiful show out of it, and it would help everyone at Saint Matthew's.

She and Dick talked about it before he left, after the TV people had gone back to Paris. He thanked her for making it happen. He was leaving in two days, and hated to go home. His heart was in Africa, with the children who needed his help.

"How long do you think you'll stay?" he asked her. It touched him that her time there meant so much to her. It had done for her what he hoped it would and brought her back to life. An even more purposeful life than she'd had before, with deeper meaning.

"I'll stay until I'm ready to go back to Paris," she said quietly. "I'm not yet. I have no purpose there anymore, no reason to go back for now." He nodded. He had understood that. She was healing here in Angola, and he was glad he had suggested she come.

The next doctor in the rotation had already arrived that day. Dick was handing over the relay to him, and filling him in on all their patients. He was another plastic surgeon, from London.

"I won't be back here again till January," he said to Véronique before he left. "Maybe you'll still be here then."

"Maybe," she said vaguely. "I have to go back sometime. I can't decide when yet." She hadn't told him that she wanted to make a large donation to the hospital, and she was going to. She had already sent Chip an email about it. He asked her how she was doing, and she said she was fine.

"You did more to heal me than anyone so far," she said to Dick, "by bringing me here."

"That's what I was hoping when I suggested it." He smiled at her.

"Your face is looking good too. I'll tell Phillip." Most of all she had learned to live with it. She hadn't even covered it with much makeup when she was on TV. What Doug had said for months had finally sunk in, and what Patrick had said when she talked to him about it. He had sent Dick an email telling him that his article had sold to the London *Sunday Times Magazine* and would be out in a few weeks.

"Well, don't stay in Africa forever," Dick told her when he left. "Come to New York to visit." But she had even less there than in Paris. She had a place to live there.

"Maybe I'll stay another month or two. I'm not ready to go back. I'd like to do what you do, and come here a few months a year. I'd like to come on your rotation."

"That's usually January through March, give or take a month."

"I might spend Christmas here. I have nowhere to be for the holiday now. This would be a good way to spend it." He nodded.

"You'll find your way again, Véronique," he assured her. "You already are. When everything falls apart like that and ends, you have to find a reason for living again. I think maybe you just did."

"I'm not so sure how great my reasons were before. It's kind of empty living off your beauty as the mainstay of your existence. I couldn't have done it forever. You don't think about things like that at eighteen or nineteen or even at twenty-three, unless something big happens to make you reevaluate your life."

"You can get involved in a project like this one, and really make a difference. Everyone loves having you here. And you helped us enormously with the television show. It will give us credibility when we ask for donations. That's all thanks to you."

She was sad to see him go the next day, and so were the others. But the doctor who took his place was young and dynamic. He'd been spending a month at Saint Matthew's for the past two years, and Véronique liked him.

She thought of going back to Paris in July, but decided to wait until the end of the summer. She had nowhere to go on vacation and no one to go with. She and her mother always went to the South of France every year, and she didn't want to go alone, or to the same place without her mother. The year before she'd still been in the hospital in Brussels. The time she had spent there had begun to seem surreal to her now, as though it had happened to someone else, a person she didn't even know anymore. She had changed so much in the last sixteen months. It took the time it took, and you couldn't control it. Angola was so beautiful. She loved it more every day. It had a kind of savage beauty, and the conditions there were hard. But the people had a gentleness and innocence that she loved. She tried to describe it to Doug in emails, but she couldn't. It spoke to her in ways that nothing ever had before.

She had found herself there after being lost for a year. She felt as though she had returned from the grave, and she didn't want to lose that again when she went back to Paris. Her life had too little meaning there, too little substance. Her mother was the glue that had held her life together and gave it depth and meaning. And now she was gone and there was nothing to replace it.

Chip had emailed her and told her he was coming to Paris in September, and she wanted to be there to see him and show him around. So she thought she'd leave at the end of August. She would have been there for four months by then. She thought maybe it was long enough for now.

She was playing with the children one night outside at sunset, and she looked up as a car drove into the compound. When it stopped, Patrick Weston got out. She was surprised to see him. He saw her right away and walked over to her, with a confident look and a warm smile.

"What are you doing here?" she asked him.

"Well, hello to you too. I told you I'd send the article. I didn't have your address, so I brought it to you." She smiled at his answer, as he took a clipping of the article out of his pocket and handed it to her. The child she'd been playing with went to find her mother, and Véronique sat down to read it. It was good and strong, and very tight, and the message clear about the good work they were doing, and the importance of ridding Angola and other countries of land mines once and for all. He mentioned seeing her there, working as a volunteer, and there were no pictures of her, just as he had promised. She was still wondering why he had come back.

"How've you been?" he asked her.

"I've been good, really good. Busy here." She smiled at him. She looked peaceful and healthy, better than when he'd last seen her. So did he. "I've been rethinking my life and what matters to me now. I still haven't figured out a job," she said, as they watched the sunset together. "Even if my life magically went back to the way it was before, I don't think I could lead that life anymore. It was heady stuff and fun, exciting and flattering. But a whole existence spent on your looks isn't very fulfilling. My mother pointed that out to me, and I ignored her. At eighteen and nineteen it was fun, and I never questioned it."

"Why would you? You were making a fortune as a top model. What girl wouldn't want that? It's every young girl's dream."

"It's a pretty empty dream, though. I'm going back to Paris in a few weeks. I think I'll come back here for a month or two every year and volunteer. But I have to find a real job now, or I'm going to bore myself to death, and everyone I know." She felt ready to see her old friends now. She felt whole again, more than ever before. Saint Matthew's and the people she met there, and the children had done that for her.

"You didn't bore me, when I met you," he said, watching her. "What kind of job?"

"I don't know, something in philanthropy, like finding other projects like this, and giving them money or raising funds for them. My father left me some that I'd like to do something useful with, to honor him and my mother. I think they'd like that." She had said as much to Chip, and he thought it was a good idea. He had told her she could start a foundation in both their names. "What about you? What have you been up to?" She was trying to seem casual about it. She was glad to see him.

"Same as you. Trying to figure things out." He looked better than when she'd last seen him and his eyes didn't look so sad. "I have this crazy idea that if I survived, there was a reason for it. I don't know what that is yet, but I know it's there somewhere. Maybe I should write a book about the November attacks in Paris, or terrorism in general, and how pervasive that is. I lost a wife and unborn child. I don't want that forgotten, about them or any of the victims. I want people to remember her and how wonderful she was. She was a writer, so I think she'd like that. I feel like we have an obligation to pay back as survivors. It's not just good enough to live through it, whether the scars are inside or out, but it's important to do something, like what you're doing here. And if you survive, you have to crawl your way back. I've been doing that for twenty months, and you for almost as long."

"All I've figured out is that life is about more than having a beautiful face. That isn't enough. It's not a reason for living, just so others can look at you. I want to be more than that," she said.

"You already are," he said quietly. "I learned something from you when I was here two months ago. Your life gets all blown to bits, the way ours did, or in some smaller way, and you have to put it all back together and find a reason for living when things change. I couldn't find that reason. You did, you found it here, and you had the guts to go looking for it.

"When I got back to London, I realized that maybe I had found it here too, and I didn't even see it. I came back to find out if the answer for me was here, and I missed it. Just like when you looked in the mirror after Brussels, all you saw were the scars. The scars aren't what it's about, or even the perfect face. It's about what's inside you and who you are. You're beautiful, Véronique, in all the ways that matter. Scars, no scars, it's irrelevant. Beauty is in the sunsets here, in the children, in the smiling faces, in the work they're doing here at Saint Matthew's. It's in your eyes, and all the people who survived the hell we lived through. We survived. Maybe that's the whole point, and the real question is what we're going to do about it. I came back here to see you," he said honestly. He didn't want to play games with her, or hide. "I've never known anyone like you, not because of your face, but because of your heart. Your heart and the love in you balances out the hatred and the horror of what happened to us. I looked at you and I knew I was alive again, so here I am," he said softly, and reached for her hand. They held hands as they watched the sun go down and sink behind the African horizon. They had found peace in Angola, and a reason for living, and they had to find a way to take it home with them, keep the flame alive and protect it against the forces of evil.

She realized that that was what her father had been telling her, never to let that go or let the flame go out. Her mother had understood that better than he had.

"I knew that if I didn't come back to see you, and let the chance go by, I'd regret it forever, and I'd think about it one day when I'm old and be sorry." He smiled at her. "So I'm here. My scars are on the inside, and they're no prettier than yours. Yours are more honest, because you can see them, you wear them like a badge of courage. I've been afraid to live again ever since that night in Paris."

"So have I," she admitted. "I thought my life ended in Brussels. I wanted it to. But it didn't. Our punishment was that we had to live without them. We tried to bury ourselves too. You after Paris, and me after Brussels. Thank you for coming back," she whispered to him, holding tightly to his hand. "You were brave to come back."

"Thank you for being here." He smiled at her. They were both present and alive, for the first time in over a year.

They had found life again in Africa. She was ready to go home and start living again. No matter how scarred inside and out, she was still beautiful. She saw it in his eyes, and she believed him. Just as he believed now that love had not died in Paris. It would come again. They had survived, and discovered in the end that life with all its beauty and tragedy and terror at times was worth living after all.

Life is beautiful, and nothing could change that, scars and all.

About the Author

DANIELLE STEEL has been hailed as one of the world's best-selling authors, with almost a billion copies of her novels sold. Her many international bestsellers include *High Stakes, Invisible, Flying Angels, The Butler, Complications, Nine Lives, Finding Ashley, The Affair, Neighbors,* and other highly acclaimed novels. She is also the author of *His Bright Light,* the story of her son Nick Traina's life and death; *A Gift of Hope,* a memoir of her work with the homeless; *Expect a Miracle,* a book of her favorite quotations for inspiration and comfort; *Pure Joy,* about the dogs she and her family have loved; and the children's books *Pretty Minnie in Paris* and *Pretty Minnie in Hollywood.*

daniellesteel.com
Facebook.com/DanielleSteelOfficial
Twitter: @daniellesteel
Instagram: @officialdaniellesteel

About the Type

This book was set in Charter, a typeface designed in 1987 by Matthew Carter (b. 1937) for Bitstream, Inc., a digital type-foundry that he cofounded in 1981. One of the most influential typographers of our time, Carter designed this versatile font to feature a compact width, squared serifs, and open letterforms. These features give the typeface a fresh, highly legible, and unencumbered appearance.